The Numismatist's Wife

Dahlia Japhet

Archway Publishing books may be ordered through booksellers or by contacting:

Archway Publishing
1663 Liberty Drive
Bloomington, IN 47403
www.archwaypublishing.com
1 (888) 242-5904

ISBN: 978-1-4808-5804-6 (sc)
ISBN: 978-1-4808-5802-2 (hc)
ISBN: 978-1-4808-5803-9 (e)

Library of Congress Control Number: 2018903214

Print information available on the last page.

Archway Publishing rev. date: 02/18/2019

We had what the others
All crave and seek for;
We left it behind at nineteen.

Gary Snyder
Four Poems for Robin

But this was something terrible. Two or three men already in the wagon
are feebly hoisting up the next man like a dead, inert body, who is barely
hanging on moaning....

S.A. An-sky
January 18, 1915
Diary of 1915

In memory of Zvi Henri Ravon z"l (1933-2013), and of my extended family, who perished in the Holocaust

1

June 20, 1999

Dana Newman woke, put aside her cotton nightgown, and dressed soundlessly. Her husband, Gerson, would probably sleep until ten. She glanced at her watch, it was nearly six a.m. She always liked Sunday mornings. She grabbed her sunhat, her small helipad, and drove north on Route 9 to Stormville. Soon she was sleuthing at the flea market, among the early buyers. She didn't feel lonely as she walked, randomly examining books, shifting watercolors, her hands sweeping over figurines, clocks, vintage clothes, woven rugs. So many possibilities—the beginning of a story, but she did not know that yet.

Her large sunhat slid off and she brushed hair out of her eyes and rearranged herself. Across the sky two eagles soared and around her people looked up, pointed to a nest. In front of Dana a tall burly man hoisted his daughter to see the eagles and the girl squealed with delight. Dana was short; between man and girl she lost sight of the eagles. She moved away, reached a corner stand and gently trailed her fingers over a jumble of beaded bags, old cameras and tea cups.

"That's a great hat, where did you get it?" the seller asked, drawing Dana closer to her stand.

"Here, a few weeks ago, maybe you know her, Jan's hats?"

"Thanks. I'll definitely look her up. If you're interested in anything from the display case, let me know."

Among rings, heavy platinum chains, intricate figure eight chains and filigree necklaces, Dana spied a cluster ring. She wondered about the owners. Where, when, why.

She tried on a few rings, a pretty garnet one with an elegant setting had a fifty dollar tag. Dana still had to roam the flea market, so spending even forty right away was too much.

"I'll come back." Nearby she saw an Oriental chest with mother of pearl inlay, *How I would like that*, she thought, casting her eye over a chair with stenciled flowers. *That would look so great in the bedroom.*

They didn't need furniture so she continued to another jewelry booth. Mixed among the cameos in a display case, Dana noticed a necklace, a medallion or a coin, on a simple chain. The coin was attractive; it had dark toning and lovely style. She asked if she might try it on.

The seller put the piece in Dana's hand and took out a mirror, "It's a unique piece."

Dana quivered with excitement and apprehension, wondering if she would be able to wrap up the transaction. This might not be a bargain. "How much?" she mouthed.

The woman peeled Dana's fingers from the necklace and dangling it beside a magnifying glass, said "Two hundred. Cash. The coin is valuable. You noticed it right away. It's an ancient coin, ordinarily more than a thousand dollars. But as you see under a magnifier, it's damaged by a long scratch. The holing reduces its value, too. Would you like to know about the coin? I don't usually get ancient coins like this. It's from about 200 B.C. It's Greek, I think. Beautiful, isn't it? Look at yourself in the mirror."

Dana gasped; it was more than she had ever spent at one outing. The seller suggested an art deco necklace, but Dana was transfixed by the ancient coin, it looked stunning on her.

What a plunge for Dana to spend so much at once. A great deal of money when she and Gerson had given up luxuries, were not eating at nice restaurants or buying expensive gifts.

"Maybe you can find a coin specialist, there must be a coin club near you, and, if you are interested in the coin, you can get information there."

Other women, regulars, Dana recognized their faces, approached the booth. A woman wearing an amazing African fabric necklace embraced a tall woman with a Gibson girl hair style, "Find anything special yet?"

Another regular, Dede from the grocery store, joined them, "That's a great sunhat," she said to Dana. "I need something like that to protect my skin."

The seller, whom they called Karen, said, "Let's go together later and find vintage hats, Dede."

The woman with the bright African necklace asked Karen, "Billy home for the summer?"

"Driving me nuts, sleeps till four p.m. Don't know where he goes nights. Having him home is something!"

They all admired the coin necklace, Dede telling a few anecdotes about coin forgeries from overseas, "They're difficult to spot," she said.

The tall woman said, "You know Assemblyman Adams? His wife always wears a smashing coin necklace."

With a girlish, almost apologetic smile, Dana whispered to Karen, "One hundred fifty?"

"One hundred eighty," and the exchange was made, in cash. Karen put the necklace in a velvet pouch and handed Dana her card, in case she had a change of heart.

The tall woman, whose wrinkles were chiseled in her face, said, "I should have gotten here at seven a.m. The only way to buy good stuff is to come early." Turning to Dana she continued, "If you want to sell it, here's my phone number," and she too handed Dana a card. She owned the antique store in Fishkill, she said. Dana had their cards, and maybe new friends.

Having spent a small fortune, she left the flea market, jaunty and pleased. She thought, *I'll call the library Monday*. Something new to research.

A stop at the supermarket, she'd be home by ten.

Winding and steep, Canopus Hill Road borders the Appalachian Trail. Beyond are woods, at the edge of which prairie warblers and wood thrushes nest. The shady side of the road is wild and overgrown with a wall of hedges and brush. Lilac and magnolia trees struggle to grow on the sunny side of the dirt road.

Former summer cabins, now winterized, inhabit the sunny side and one of these, fronted by a stream, is the Newmans' house. Three barking sheepdogs disturb the stillness when they hear hikers or cars crest the hill.

As she drove up Dana heard the dogs, expected they would block the entrance, stubbornly waiting for a game of ball or flying squirrel. They always did that.

"We have food till next year," Gerson said, as they both carried the groceries into the house.

Gerson had tidied the kitchen and living area. It still looked shabby, had too much furniture, all too heavy for this small cottage. Gerson always helped with the groceries; he wanted to be useful. He was always right behind her, a pace away, trying to please her.

Dana went over to the table and opened her pouch, extending the necklace toward him.

"What do you think?"

Loudly crunching an apple— it would have been better if he had cut it in fourths—he almost had his sticky fingers on the coin, "I can't see much of it, but I like the chain. It's not very clean, is it?"

"Someone said I can't just clean it with soap or a pad. I need to find an expert."

Like a mountain lion, Gerson roared, interested now, "I – my cousin Paul. Paul Eddings would know."

"The cousin whom your brothers say was so underhanded in the family's restitution lawsuit?"

Suddenly Dana felt something would happen in their lives now, she just knew it. Gerson felt it too, because he was unusually excited, was speaking quickly, in staccato phrases.

"Paul's my first cousin. Ilse was my aunt. My cousin Paul's mother. Paul collects coins, there's a term for that."

It was not too clear to Dana, "What on earth are you saying? Did your aunt have a necklace like this?" She bent down in front of him so that the pendant touched his nose.

He was following his own train of thought, "Ilse was my mother's sister."

"She had a necklace like this?" Dana startled Gerson, put her hand a bit too roughly on his shoulder, and he almost tripped, moving away.

"Maybe. Paul is a collector. Like his father. I haven't talked to him in many years. He lives nearby, In White Plains, I think."

"He lives near us and we never spoke to him?" she asked. She's been so lonely and she doesn't care about the lawsuit. The necklace might be a bridge to other people, a connection to other lives.

For a few days, squatting in the garden, hair tangled with roots and grass, pruning and weeding, Dana thought about Paul and Ilse and coins. She asked Gerson about his family but he reluctantly brushed off her questions. She learned there was a numismatic society, called their librarian and shared her newfound knowledge with Gerson, who listened with a careworn smile.

"Let's call him," she said one day.

"Who?" Gerson replied.

"Your cousin, Paul."

Gerson settled back, "I haven't talked to him in many years. My brother kept in touch with him."

"So what? Let's try."

Reluctantly he agreed to call though he felt awkward and apprehensive about meeting people. He had forgotten the jokes and anecdotes he used to tell so easily.

"It's Gerson Newman," he said with a gravelly voice.

2

June-July 1999

Paul Eddings had last seen Gerson Newman at a small gathering in the New York City apartment of Gerson's oldest brother, a banker widely recognized for being distinguished and loud. That occasion brought together couples who had family ties stretching back to Germany. Unlike Gerson, an engineer, most had become bankers—Paul had been an international banker in Rome. Now nineteen summers later, they were meeting in the restaurant at the Rye Hilton with their wives. Although excursions exhausted Paul, they obviously pleased Rachel, his wife, whom he referred to in his wry, witty way as "the government."

Rachel was both the archivist and the librarian presiding over the learned chaos of the Eddingses' apartment. Their movements were restricted by books, coins, medals, books about coins and medals, etchings, and family memorabilia. Their collection was valuable and they were considering donating it to the right museums and universities. They took coins out from their safety-deposit box, reviewed their history, catalogued them, and shared memories regarding the purchase of a particular coin, who had auctioned it, and when they bought it. Often, they laughed at a foolish, impetuous purchase and at forgeries they had bought. They also invested in rare books and had a first-class numismatic library. They had become more critical as their collection grew and were now nostalgically embarrassed by a misjudgment, a beautiful coin they had not bought when it was offered privately to them, when ancient

Greek coins had not fit neatly into their collection. Later, it fetched a majestic price at auction, which made for a good story, the kind of story every collector has.

As methodically as he kept his coins, Paul kept lists of friends and relatives. Gerson had arrived in New York some twenty years after Paul; he married, divorced, remarried his wife, then divorced again. After this second divorce, just after that small gathering in 1980, Paul and Rachel had phoned him, invited him for dinner, he had refused.

Now, nineteen years later, when they had almost forgotten him, Gerson had phoned them. He didn't remember refusing invitations or the gathering. He volunteered, "I don't live in Scarsdale now. I moved to Putnam Valley; that was five years ago."

"Where?"

"Putnam Valley—it's semicivilized, and we don't milk many cows." He still had his sense of humor. "I remarried — Dana's the right one," he continued wryly. "She asked me to phone you, it's something about a coin, can we meet?"

Gerson's family ties were mostly with his daughter, he said. Except for his daughter he rarely spoke to anyone but Dana. He wasn't following the lawsuit —they agreed not to discuss it and settled on dinner in July.

It was a breezy summer afternoon. Off Ridge Road, Rachel Eddings pinned her brooch to her scarf, Paul fixed his bow tie, although for the Rye Hilton, that wasn't necessary. "I'm quite pleased we shall meet Gerson again," he said. "He always seemed sad, so introverted around other people."

"We've been lucky, haven't we?" Rachel kissed Paul on the cheek. "We've had a good life together. Let's make sure we haven't forgotten to turn the gas off," she laughed. "After all, we are old."

"You mean I am; you're still in your young seventies. Did I tell you I like your new hairstyle? It's very becoming," Paul returned the kiss.

"Oh, we're two old people encircled by books." She pointed to their library. "We can't even reach most of them anymore; the terrace is full of books too. I'm glad the landlord started fixing problems in the building;

for so many years it was shabby with strange people renting here." As Rachel and Paul went down the elevator, she said, "There are still too many dogs, though."

The Eddingses were always on time, *pünktlich*. They waited outside their building a couple of minutes. Dana brought the Durango up to the curb, waving energetically. She jumped out to meet Gerson's cousin, she was confident she looked pretty, even lovely, in a spaghetti strap dress.

She helped the Eddingses, although they managed to place their feet properly on the running board and were quite agile. Paul remarked they had had a Lexus that they parked in someone else's garage which had been stolen. They really didn't need a car, living close to King's Road. Dana thought how wonderful it was to live so simply. That's how it is with people who amass a fortune; they rent a one-bedroom, not worrying about taxes and repairs.

Dana looked at the people around her. Her husband, Gerson, had thick gray hair, an angular, once beautiful face, but his formerly eloquent eyes, although still lively, were almost emptied of expression. His hair was unruly though she had slicked some cream on, and he looked awkward in a new seersucker suit.

Paul, in his mid to late eighties, was dignified with thin black hair; Rachel was so agreeable and so very attractive for her age, impeccable in a navy blue pantsuit with a charming scarf. Retired, the Eddingses spent their time with friends and family. Rachel especially was fascinated meeting new people, everyone was a novel, she said.

The two couples formed one of those remarkable contrasts that waiters are trained to ignore. Perhaps that very day, other equally strange couples were dining up and down Route 1 and on Westchester Avenue.

Rachel had a delighted smile as she said to Dana, "*Wenn Engel reisen, weint der Himmel.* Do you understand that? My family would say that for *bon voyage.* Being in your truck was like going on a moon voyage for us."

Dana said, "I'm sorry, I didn't study German. Maybe I will try. My language in college was Russian. Studying Russian was very popular then."

Dana soon settled on her most comfortable subject, one about which Paul and Rachel had no idea at all. She described her sheepdogs, how, when sad, she burrowed her face in their long, thick coats. Some weekends she drove them to New Jersey for herding lessons, which she also described. Rachel and Paul listened in wonder as this petite, middle-aged woman, choosing between apple cake and Bavarian cream with strawberries, carried on a monologue about dogs.

Dana was attached to the dogs, to cats, chickens, and the occasional hamster. She described the glories of magenta sunsets viewed from a high deck and the overall peace and quiet of her life. It seemed that for human friendship she had only Gerson. She took out some photos.

"These are the dahlias and roses blooming in our garden now. Perhaps," she added, turning to Rachel, "we can have you over sometime and show off."

"A lovely pastoral life," Rachel said.

"Mostly, yes. Although not in winter—I prefer to remain home to driving in snow for food shopping. This time of the year the garden has to be protected from Japanese beetles and slugs. Sometimes I think it should be left wild."

Paul was talking to Gerson. "How well I remember your parents' blue room. It was a fine example of Biedermeier, with the armoire at the entrance."

Gerson, though he never spoke of it, remembered his childhood and his parents. His memories turned to Annette, his mother, sitting on the sofa, a study in shadows. When Gerson's father, Martin, was successful they moved to Saint Anna Platz in Munich. In the blue room, their parents would hug them and read to them. For Gerson, that room had been home and warmth; the blue room, with its piano, the hand-carved tables, the tapestry, and the yellow sofa, was still vivid to him. There were paintings in elaborate frames, and craftsmen had even produced hand-beaded frames for Annette, in which academic portraits by Kauffman and Menzel were hung. Wearing shoes was strictly forbidden in the blue room.

"Let's talk more with our tea, on the patio," Paul said.

The waiter came over. Dana considered the list of possibilities—did she want coffee? Hot chocolate? Tea? She could not risk behaving like a country cousin. "Yes, yes. Tea will be perfect." She was an avid coffee drinker, yet somehow she had said rosehips tea.

While they waited for the beverages, Dana imagined the room both men remembered so vividly, with a youthful Annette playing the piano and singing Lieder, as something very Germanic.

"I met Annette," Dana said. "She was amazing. Her mind was so sharp, even at ninety-one." She remembered the orderly apartment on King George Street in Jerusalem where the ancient lady kept laces and multiple sets of dishes and monogrammed silver. She thought, *I wish I had such items to sell at a flea market.*

Gerson said, "We were three wild boys. When we moved to an Arab quarter in Palestine, in 1933, my mother could not control us. Then she learned to frighten us if she spoke about your mother, Paul. She told us Ilse abandoned you. We did not ask questions. In my nightmares, my parents abandoned me. Until I was ten, darkness frightened me, and a light had to be near my bed."

Slightly agitated at the memory, Gerson picked up a teaspoon of sugar, but his tea hadn't arrived. When it did, he drank it unsweetened. They all had a good natured laugh and finished dessert. Paul said, "Let me take this one. We invited you here."

When they moved to the patio, Dana took out her treasure, putting it on a table napkin. Paul, who brought his loupe, examined the coin, saying, "A very fine example of this coin would be a marvel, these coins circulated a lot. This one is definitely worth at least $300, despite that scratch. If you hold the loupe to your eye and look closely you can see that the style is Greek, though it's a Roman coin. It's one of my favorites and there's no need to clean it unless you want the relief to be more vivid. This didrachm is thought to be one of the first silver coins struck in Rome, struck around 266 B.C. It's safe for you to remove the encrustation with water and a soft toothbrush. Since you aren't selling it, I wouldn't involve a professional cleaner right now. It will look nice enough as a necklace. You can phone me if you have questions, of course. You know what? I have such a didrachm, in good condition. I'll show it to you when we meet again. Our coins aren't at home, you see, they're in a bank vault."

Dana said, "Thank you, Paul. For everything. I would very much like to hear about your family. Gerson is so reticent. Did your mother have necklaces like this?"

"One particular necklace, yes. My father's first gift to her was a necklace with a Roman coin. The coin's style was different. If you're interested and want to learn about ancient coins, I can start you off with some material."

"Great, great. Your father was also a coin collector?"

"My father, Georg, was a scholar and collector of ancient coins. Even now I feel him lifting me on a chair so I could look through the microscope – my first sightings of coins magnified. I loved him and standing there, still wearing a crisp sailor suit, I noticed distinguishing marks, scratches, overstrikes on coins. He said I had a gift for coin collecting, a wonderful memory—and he would teach me to identify Greek and Roman coins by their inscriptions."

Paul leaned closer, "You don't stop grieving for such parents— it's comforting to tell their story."

Rachel said, "We'll get together next month. We'll show you some very fine coins from our collection."

Excitement spun in Dana's stomach. She was overjoyed that they had a shared purpose—the four of them.

3

March 1912

Over and over, Ilse turned in her sleep, dreaming of dancing blue horses; she was a voyeur and a participant in her own dream. Intensely blue horses surged ahead, nostrils flaring. She was running with them, straining for their thundering hooves, as an orange gold figure came into focus. She heard the flick-flack of the Bavarian flag with the royal Wittelsbach blue color and saw the cobblestones of the Marienplatz and the great clock with the clashing red and green knights. She ran fiercely, trying to catch the horses and the spectral rider.

At dawn, as news peddlers were still collecting their papers, she woke startled and looked out the window. *It will be a sunny day*, she thought, though a thick fog hung in the air. She wanted to embrace everything: the street, her neighbors, and the birds flocking to the windowsill.

Still conscious of the dream—the rough form of the red rider, the horse changing to a deep blue, muscular, splendid in motion—Ilse decided to write her step-cousin Georg. At nineteen, he was two years older than she was, and had just passed his Abitur examinations. She wrote that the powerful stallions flowed with the rider, as if they were one, and that the dream made her feel strange, she couldn't define the feeling. She had a small desk by her bed, and she kept Georg's letters there. She liked to read all of them several times, but especially his last letter, brought to her by a family friend, left her eager and excited to see him. Lightheaded, she had read it six times, and she took it out now to read again.

"I'm at the peak of my fencing now," he had written, *"and just won in a tournament 15–9. I stayed calm during the bout, which was the main thing. My opponent, a schoolmate who received the Abitur with me, suggested I join the army. He is beginning officer training at the academy, and I shall apply. What do you think? My best news is that I went to a coin dealer last week and bought twenty great coins! I wish you could see them.*

"Sweet Ilse, I think of you several hours a day, and am enclosing a gift for you, a silver denarius with the head of Apollo. It's a nice coin, and I've mounted it in a bezel, with a chain. I imagine you wearing it around your lovely neck. The denarius will look perfect on you. I wait to hear how you like it, and wait to see you and kiss your cheek."

Laureate head of Apollo

She had seen Apollo in sculptures, in marble and bronze, and viewed his painful longing for Daphne in a painting at the Pinakothek gallery. She went up to her mirror and slipping the necklace over her head, swayed as if she and Georg were dancing, kissed the air, and with the letter, necklace and mirror, moved from side to side. *I need to think of a gift for him, too, perhaps the painting of the horse in my dreams. Or maybe of Apollo, as the Roman god of victory, or as a sun god. I know he will tell me all about the coin he gave me, where it was struck, and where he bought it. Then we'll go for a walk, he'll be the Apollo to my Daphne, and I shall pretend to run away. But I won't, for I do like him so. Luckily I am short and we are just right together, we could dance down Rosenbuschstrasse!*

Rosenbuschstrasse was a stylish street, off the regal main thoroughfare, with elegant apartment houses. The façade of number eight, her family's residence, had ornate ironwork gates, sculpted Atlases supporting the balconies, and caryatids adorning the door knockers. Climbing roses, reaching the top of the gates, seemed to announce that within that home there was youthful sensual beauty and delight. In summer, when chairs were placed around the apple and beech trees, the courtyard attracted the residents. Even when it was cold, Ilse would sometimes run down to the courtyard just to experience the crisp winter air.

The week before, Ilse helped Hedwig, her mother, by serving at a dinner party. Her father, Moshe Ehrenkrantz, raised a whiskey glass. "Gentlemen, let us toast our bankers, Bleichröder and Strauss."

His friends responded, "Hurrah! Hurrah!"

A slightly older friend, bald, holding a gold lorgnette, said, "The only reason the Reichstag is pandering to Jews and giving us new privileges is because of the power of our bankers."

"No, Ezra, there is a new atmosphere in Germany. You can read for yourself a condemnation of anti-Semitic sermons in the recent *Vossische Zeitung.*"

"Yes, you are right—in a peripheral article on the fifth page!" Ezra retorted.

"Do you know, in my village of Bialobrzegi, if a Pole coming down the road encountered a Jew, he could insist that the Jew get out of the way and into the ditch? Or he could bludgeon the Jew. That does not happen here. We are part of the Reich. My children," Moshe continued, "hold their heads high. We can have our Torah and our prayers and participate in this great culture."

So saying, Moshe raised his glass again, "Let us toast the health of the Kaiser."

On Friday night, the Ehrenkrantz family assembled for Shabbos dinner. Moshe blessed his sons, Walther, already a young man of twenty-two, and Leon, who was just entering university. "May God make you like Ephraim and Menashe." He placed his hands on their heads as he said the blessing.

Then Hedwig blessed Ilse, now seventeen, and her younger sister,

Annette. "May God make you like Sarah, Rebecca, Rachel, and Leah, who together built up the family of Israel."

Annette, who was quite tall, lowered her head.

Before the Friday night Kiddush, the family sang "Eishet Chayil, a Woman of Valor" in unison, reminding Hedwig of her worth; every time she heard the song, she was touched and, blushing, warmly kissed her husband and then her children. In between courses, the men sang traditional songs and the women harmonized. They sang "L'cha Dodi" and "Shalom Aleichem." They pounded the rhythm on the table, and Ilse and Annette danced in place, either holding hands with their mother or clapping in time.

Later, Moshe said, "If it's fine on Sunday, we'll go for a walk in the English Garden."

Ilse jumped at the idea. "Surely there will be a horse guard parade!"

"Showmanship!" Leon stammered. "Germany's militarism." Moshe and Hedwig didn't like this kind of talk, but no one challenged Leon— Leon the pacifist, the socialist. It was Shabbos and there would be no friction at their Shabbos table.

On Saturdays, when he joined fellow Jewish merchants and bankers at the Central Synagogue, Moshe Ehrenkrantz, like the other men, wore a black suit and top hat. Walther attended synagogue on Friday nights, on Saturdays, and also during the week. Moshe, who had grown up in the Jewish community of Bialobrzegi, no longer swayed during prayer, while Walther adopted the Orthodox conventions of chanting, bending, and even prostrating himself for some prayers.

As the men returned to the apartment, Walther took his father's arm. "The Rabbi's lesson today was absorbing. The dramatic episode of Rabbi Elisha ben Abuyah, who rebelled against God, is full of awe and dread. Does it seem possible that, despite being a great Torah scholar, despite Rabbi Meir's continual urging, after hearing a heavenly condemnation precluding him from repenting, Elisha, according to the Babylonian tradition, would not repent?"

"Our Rabbi's talk about the Jerusalem Talmudic interpretation was to the point," replied Moshe. "Rabbi Elisha laments the suffering of righteous people. He laments the death of a good man and the suffering of Rabbi Judah the Baker. Because their suffering is incomprehensible to him, he refuses to repent. When his student, the sage Rabbi Meir, visits him on his deathbed, Rabbi Elisha weeps before dying. Rabbi Meir teaches us that Elisha was redeemed by his tears and knowledge of Torah. So our rabbi teaches us that a Jew may always repent, even at the very end of life."*

In the parlor, Ilse said, "It will be nice tomorrow. Surely we can go to the English Garden." She kissed her father and twirled around the apartment in new gloves and a new cap until the family sat down for the Shabbos meal.

Although it was March, Sunday was warm and the streets were a carnival of colors and hues, as shopkeepers mingled with actors, peddlers with bankers, and students with politicians. The park was crowded, and it was difficult to find a quiet spot. Young boys in sailor suits and young girls in long dresses with starched white collars ran to watch a puppet show. Moshe sought out a favorite spot where he could tell legends to his daughters.

"Oh Papa, I so want to see the puppet show and then the cavalry show," a restless Ilse said.

Over and over, the image of the blue horses returned to her. She thought about the rider. She thought about the rider and then about Georg, her red headed cousin; he had such soft, flowing hair. She often thought of the promises they made as children and the secrets they shared with more than just affection.

"Am I repeating stories you've already heard?" Moshe pretended to be hurt. "Go ahead, and I shall just sit here alone and weep!"

"I know," Ilse said, "that you'll soon be in a deep political conversation, while we watch Kasperl and the parade."

---

* *Rabbinic Stories*, translated by Jeffrey L. Bernstein, part IX, "Sin and Repentance," pages 229–244. Also *Elisha ben Abuyah*, translated by David J. Halperin, https://*www.davidhalperin.net*/wp-content/uploads/2013/05/Elisha-Stories.pdf.

While the puppets tussled, Ilse said to Annette, "Mama is right, you know. You should apply to the conservatory. You have a talent for the piano, and you'd learn new things there."

"Yes," Annette said, "I'm sure you're right, but I don't want to leave home. Not now, not yet. Soon it will be spring, and I can prepare our little rose garden."

Tactfully, Ilse said, "Our roses really are the most beautiful and everyone admires them. But seriously, you need to advance; you don't want to remain here tending roses."

"Nonsense," Annette replied. "I love music, but I am also happy the way I am. I don't feel a need to change, to set myself into a new mold."

Ilse did not say it, but she knew that her sister was afraid of leaving her sheltered home; Annette clung to their mother when she was anxious. Ilse thought it best not to dwell on this, so she said, half joking,

"I hope you are not doing this to be with Claude."

"Maybe that too. I am sure he is handsomer than the conservatory professors. Why do you bother? I allot certain hours each day to the piano, and I don't neglect any other tasks. Perhaps next year I'll go to another school. You're the one who flirts with Claude when he comes to give me my piano lesson. You're the one who laughs and calls him a shaggy dog, playing with his hair."

"I think," Ilse said, "you're just determined to have all your music lessons with Claude."

Annette wanted to change the subject. "Do you realize what great blessings we have? Papa's brother died of consumption in their village; Mama's grandparents were poor Westphalian farmers. Our parents created a grand life for us. That's why Papa has such a positive, optimistic attitude. He is not very concerned when he hears sneers about Jews."

"Annette, you surely have strange ideas. Let's talk about May. Georg is coming from Berlin, and we shall have a great trip—somewhere. Will you come too? I hear a charming young bachelor is also coming from Hamburg."

"Then you bicycle with this Prince Charming, and I will ride alone with Georg," Annette said snippily.

While the sisters provoked each other, Moshe discussed Bethmann-Hollweg's latest political moves and railroad bonds with some associates. Sam Liebermann, a wealthy businessman, joined the group with his wife, Sara. In contrast to the maidenly clothes Annette and Ilse wore, Sara wore a pansy-colored cloak, the folds falling gracefully around her draped figure. When Herr Liebermann and his now deceased wife, Klara, met Sara, she had been a milliner's assistant speaking Yiddish and Russian. There were rumors that when the thirty day mourning period for Klara ended, Herr Liebermann sought Sara out and financed her German lessons. Within a year they were married. Moshe's acquaintances said Sara was the most beautiful hostess in Munich and regretted that she rarely socialized outside her home. At thirty-six, she was too old, she thought, to meet young couples and too young to warm to the matrons. As Liebermann was very influential, even well connected with the Warburgs in Hamburg, the most important industrialists and officials came to his parties. Sometimes he held parties on Shabbos and Orthodox Jews were, of necessity, or perhaps purposely, excluded. In the Herzog Maxstrasse Synagogue, there was some resentment toward Liebermann. Many would have liked to see his downfall, but not Moshe, who had made a lot of money with Liebermann's advice. He had taken profits out of his company and put them in railroad bonds, and the gains were impressive. The Ehrenkrantz Press turned a profit, yet without this windfall, he would never have rented two floors on Rosenbuschstrasse, in the best section of Munich.

"Look, Ilse, at the brim of Sara's hat! Will we ever wear such elegant clothes?"

"Maybe, Annette, if we run toward our dreams and not away from them. Maybe we will marry fine bankers! Who knows—"

The sisters heard Sam Liebermann saying, "Herr Ehrenkrantz, you need to take an interest in politics too. If we have to pay higher wages to our workers, we'll all be undone. Do join us at our party next week. Director von Rieppel of Maschinenfabrik was invited, and he is considered an excellent speaker. The party will be on a Thursday, and we would like to see you."

"How lovely if you and Mrs. Ehrenkrantz would join us," Sara chimed in. "We will also be celebrating Dorothea's birthday, and we would be delighted if you would bring your family. Of course, the gentlemen will talk politics and business, but this is also a ball. Invitations will be hand-delivered tomorrow."

Sara's black silky hair was piled high. There was a perfect line from the nape of her neck to her hair, and she wore a modest hat whose plumes, rather than swept forward as was the current style, were fashioned to lightly touch her neck, accentuating the collar with its glass beads on her cloak. Sara extended her green-gloved hand to Moshe who, glancing about uncomfortably, shook her hand rather than embarrass her. Despite the awkward moment, Sara remained composed, acknowledging this with a friendly, in fact, dazzling smile.

English Garden, Munich, 1908

"*Gnädige Frau*, to please you, I'll surely be there with Mrs. Ehrenkrantz," Moshe answered. "No one should doubt my loyalty to our country and to the Prince Regent. Certainly, the rants of extremist Socialists threaten the peace and harmony of Munich, and if von Rieppel the industrialist will be there, I would like to meet him. And you say he is a good speaker? If I had eloquence, I'd make patriotic speeches to my workers and my family."

Ilse and Annette weren't surprised as they listened to their father. He was the best of fathers and a humble man, but he was so enthusiastic in his patriotism that he was sometimes at risk of being a bore—perhaps slightly belligerent—at parties.

Just as the conversation was ebbing, the Ehrenkrantz girls saw Claude Bertram, the piano teacher, approaching. Dressed in a long beige coat and beret, he waved cheerfully to them and introductions were made. Confidently, Claude extended his arm toward Sara, and when she put her hand in his, he bowed courteously.

"To meet a French gentleman—and an ardent one at that—is so delightful. Just a moment; let me remove my glove," she said coyly. Gracefully, he kissed her hand.

In that instant, Ilse imagined her future, inhaled deeply, imagined that Georg was kissing her. Ilse couldn't exhale for a moment; her heart was racing, though she understood Claude's gesture was mere politeness. After all Sara had also extended her hand to Moshe. Yet there was something different now and Ilse had a surprising prickling sensation, something not felt before.

As Sara turned back to her husband, her high cheekbones revealed a slight pink flush. How different her olive skin was from that of the Ehrenkrantzes. Yet her personality was at odds with her refined appearance. Under all the poufs and glass beads, she was close to her stepdaughter, Dorothea.

As a young girl, growing up in Berdichev, Sara had often been hungry and seen destitute neighbors collapse and die. There had been no time for games and play, especially at harvest time, when she worked from dawn until past midnight. Beneath her soft green gloves were gnarled gray hands that had done peasant work and fingers cut in fields of rye.

4

March 1912

At dawn on Mondays and Thursdays, Moshe and Walther Ehrenkrantz went to morning prayers, a long service on the days of Torah reading. Before leaving, Walther and Leon helped light the coal stove. They did this for their mother's sake.

Monthly, on wintry Wednesdays, they waited for the coal delivery. They were accustomed to helping Simon Kittel with his delivery, and while they dumped coal into the chute, they discussed the federal elections, in which the Socialists had surprised everyone by doing so well.

"Equality, it's a dream, I tell you, Herr Kittel," Moshe said on this particular Wednesday, "but it's harmless enough if you voted for the Socialists—just as long as you didn't vote for Liebknecht."

Leon declared, "We should take up the slogan of the French Revolution." While he would not contradict his father, he supported Karl Liebknecht and workers' rights. "There will be a new faith, the sun will shine brightly for workers, you will see Herr Kittel, it won't be long now." Leon, almost stammering, tried to avoid disrespecting his father, but he had fixed ideas.

"Well, gentlemen, I see the families around here. I go from house to house, everywhere such waste while the ladies dress up in flounces. You and your wife aren't haughty, but some of your neighbors forget it's only an accident of birth that I deliver coal."

"You know I'm not a man of politics," Moshe said. "We were put on the earth to work and feed our families. You're a devout Catholic, and I'm an observant Jew. We both believe in God's wisdom and it hurts me to hear your bitterness."

When they closed the cellar window, their arms sore, Leon and Walther left. Moshe invited Simon into the informal parlor where, after Simon removed his jacket and a blanket was spread on the fine green leather chairs, they shared a brandy.

Moshe reflected, "Our children will not know the poverty we endured. If my daughters had grown up in my village, Bialobrzegi, they would be out doing the washing, and if they had anything in lace, it would only be for the Sabbath. May I pour you more brandy? It will warm you for the rest of your deliveries.

"I apprenticed to a printer of a Yiddish journal printed on thin paper," Moshe continued. "He had to cut corners just to print the four-page paper, and besides news, it included translations and two-page stories. The paper sold for two rubles, and the villagers passed it around, especially the women while they waited for their cholent to cook or their husbands to return from prayer. They avidly read the stories, which transported them from Bialobrzegi to a fantasy world of gowns and flounces.

"When I came to Munich, I was poor and alone, but I had the idea to print such a rag right here in this elegant, princely city. I didn't know it was a ridiculous idea, a stupid idea, and since I was starving, I stuck to it obsessively, probably in delirium, as my only hope. I met a dreamer like myself, who had some money—my wife's father. He realized there was profit in the thing, the newness of it, and we set up a small press. Then, my father-in-law, may his memory be a blessing, had the vision of a publishing house, specializing in literary works by Bavarian authors.

"Now we own over thirty presses. I was not clever. If I had understood the challenges, I would have despaired. Today, young writers whip up romances every week, fantasies involving young adventurers, traveling in jungles, conquering armies or female hearts. My daughter Ilse had the idea of writing about a female mouse traveling around the world, and then Leon created Else the mouse, our most profitable children's storyline now. Herr Kittel, I must give you some of our books for your family, as a token of friendship."

Drinking brandy made Simon sweat; beads of perspiration gathered in the creases of his face. But Simon was comfortable and not eager to leave, so Moshe went on.

"I still like the old-fashioned stories from my village," he said. "Three old rabbis are half asleep, with their prayer books open. Their wives are preparing a holiday meal when a genie appears before them and they are startled. The wife of the Odessa rabbi, Reb Nathan, invites the genie to share the meal. Then the wife of the Minsk rabbi, Reb Shmuel, invites him for cake. The third rebbetzin pours fine whiskey for him. The three rebbetzins are wrapped in rags, and the genie tells them he will give them beautiful clothes.

"At once, chiffon and lace dresses, high heels and shawls of brilliant colors appear. 'Take whatever you want, it's all for you,' the genie says. Reb Shmuel's wife throws aside her ugly burlap dress and puts on a red dress with bows across the front and a pair of high-heeled bright-red shoes. Reb Nathan's wife chooses a navy-blue gown with sequins and replaces her worn scarf with a shawl of luminescent colors. Only the third wife, she of the tight mouth with corners down, hangs back, afraid of the gems and sparkling dresses. *What would I do with such beautiful clothes?* she thinks. *I have to milk the cow, sweep the barn, and shear the lamb.*"

Like one of the rabbis of the tale, Simon was half dozing with the brandy and the sound of Moshe's baritone. Then stiffly rousing himself, Simon said, "A strange story."

"Oh, it's just the beginning of what becomes a long story. That's how we printed our paper in my small town. There was a touch of fable mixed with a bitter truth about humanity, to be skimmed in a few pages. The reader had to wait for the next paper, and the installments continued for many weeks until concluding. The genie, who then appears in other stories, tempts the villagers, both Jewish and Christian."

Simon was getting ready to go back into the cold but lingered. "Are the men tempted or just the women?"

"The men are much worse than the women. The women are tricked on externals such as clothing, but men can be turned into heretics. We are now trying out a serial magazine in our German offerings, a *Feuilletonstil*. We have young, enthusiastic writers all fired up with imagination; they're too modern for me. Walther has to subdue them occasionally. The paper would not survive without him; he controls these writers, especially the Russian writers with their fantasies of a mysterious future. How their writing sells! It's a grand mixture of religion and crime and mysticism. I make sure that my daughters, especially Ilse, the eldest, read the stories before they are published. She loves storytelling and is our best critic."

Simon was a laborer, not a tale spinner. Usually when he finished his deliveries, he went home and forgot the hard day of labor. Except for Mr. Ehrenkrantz, no one invited him in for brandy, and he was fond of this Jewish customer. He was a man of few words, and he looked forward to the dawn of Wednesdays, to Moshe with his tall stories and his son, the young reformer absurdly talking about revolutions. He had been drinking brandy there for years, even when Leon, now such a vehement socialist, barely walked. Warmed with brandy, he was ready to resume his deliveries. Moshe handed him his black wool cap and coat and a few books, and the two men shook hands. Simon left shaking his head, for he firmly believed that the bourgeoisie were a despicable lot, but how could one be angry at a man who served you brandy and entertained you with such stories?

***

The Delft tile fireplace was stoked by the cook for the women of the family. By the time Ilse reached the kitchen, the fire was warming the third-floor apartment, and Frau Zimmerl was already folding linen.

"Oh, who will kiss me?" Ilse cried in mock despair as she swept into the kitchen to join her younger sister, Annette. "Would you butter a roll for me?"

"Your Highness, butter your own roll, please," Frau Zimmerl gently reprimanded her.

"Wouldn't you, please? We might be late to school!" Ilse teased. She pulled some stray curls out of the lace caplet that Annette wore winter mornings.

"These tiles amaze me," Ilse said as she examined the fireplace. "I have looked everywhere for such a blue—it's really unique. It's not in the sky or a lake or in any fabric—the blue color glows, getting deeper as I stare at it. It's as if the craftsman had prepared it just for us, with a special touch, magic. I want my wedding dress to be this color of blue."

"More likely," Annette replied drily, pushing Ilse's hand away and tucking her curls back, "it's just the sun's reflection. You and your magic!"

Frau Zimmerl laughed. "I hope we are invited to this wedding! In the meantime, sit properly for your coffee. Here, your mother left you a copy of *Simplicissimus*."

Ilse blew a kiss to the door, as if her mother were there. *Dear Mama,* she thought, *you are a wonderful mother, so intelligent, so generous. I dreamed I would not turn out as fine as you are. I will be quite a horror!*

Except on the Sabbath, the girls did not eat in the dining room, sitting instead in the kitchen with Frau Zimmerl and sometimes with Leon, their brother. Although at eighteen, he was a year older than Ilse, Leon was small and looked boyish. Several operations had ameliorated a spine deformity, yet he limped badly. Meals were the best time for the sisters' daydreaming, for imagining they were Biblical or romance heroines. Frau Zimmerl did not discourage them. She was rather simple and did not exert much discipline.

She had a special fondness for Annette, who would always be in Ilse's shadow. Ilse gave the impression of being beautiful; the first thing one noticed was her heart shaped face. There was sweetness there, and her prominent, curved eyebrows and wide mouth with bright white teeth and a huge smile served her well. Annette was a pale reflection of her sister. Her eyebrows were thinner, her mouth smaller, and she walked with a slightly stooped posture because of her height. She was a follower, with a malleable disposition; young men would not fear her.

On cold mornings, Frau Zimmerl constantly worried whether

Annette and Ilse were dressed warmly enough for school. Were their blouses starched, their shoes polished? It was Ilse's last year in the Mädchenschule; she was already accomplished in French, art history, and piano. Annette, in her penultimate year, needed praise and encouragement. She was needy, very much in Ilse's shadow. Yet she was very musical, and Hedwig, encouraging her talent, had hired Claude Bertram, the young Frenchman studying in Munich, as a piano teacher.

In the evenings, Hedwig read in the parlor until her husband came home. At her side were some books and the monthly journal. Ilse suspected that Hedwig knew just what was going on in the house, knew when Leon left for the beer garden, knew exactly when Frau Zimmerl was dusting, warming up soup in the kitchen or chatting with the cook.

Just as soon as their dinner was over, the sisters ran into the parlor and sat beside their mother. Hedwig stroked their fine hair, admired them and praised their French. "My darlings," she seemed to be saying, "I am here to protect you. Do you know, I could not exist without you?" She observed her daughters as they riffled through her books, fingered her skirt, and fidgeted beside her.

"I am so happy when you are here, my girls," Hedwig said with touching warmth. Annette clung to her, put her arms around her mother's neck.

"How are you doing with your French?"

Ilse took her mother's cigarette. "Ooh la, la, Claude," she replied, pretending to smoke. "Annette *l'adore*!"

"My dear Ilse," her mother said, "I don't think Annette loves Claude, though if I were her age, I might be infatuated with him. He's not only handsome, he's a very decent young man, a serious young man who makes sure not to get involved with such silly *Mädchen*. I will be proud when you love someone completely. Certainly, I shall never make fun of you! Now Ilse, you have wet the end of my cigarette."

"Oh, Mama, do use the cigarette holder. You look like a perfect spy with it," Ilse pleaded.

"All right," Hedwig said, taking the long filigree holder from a nearby nesting table. "You may each have a puff. Too bad we have no red color here for your noses, you clowns, now off you go."

They inhaled, coughed, and then ran hand in hand to do their homework.

Ilse turned to her sister. "Do you remember Mama's story that when we were little, Frau Zimmerl was engaged to the coalman? I wonder what happened."

"Shh," Annette said.

"I would like to know. Mama says Frau Zimmerl was attractive, with enormous eyes. She must have been heartbroken! It's very important, don't you see? I'd like to know about her girlhood, her Catholic upbringing, why she rarely crosses herself, and especially if she loved us when we were little as much as she did the coalman."

"Aren't you being egotistical?" Annette taunted.

"And I wonder about the coalman and his feelings for her and if he was passionate then. I'm glad she's with us but sad, too, she deserves her own family. How did their relationship end?"

Annette said, "Shush, it's probably boring."

"Oh Annette, the young Frau Zimmerl was not boring, she was like us, skipping home, longing for a beau!"

At dusk, lights came on in the homes on Franz-Josef-Strasse, on Wilhelmstrasse, by the Isar, and on Rosenbuschstrasse, as Frau Zimmerl put the clean, folded sheets away. She looked at her arthritic hands and was glad that they were still useful. She could not open the coal chute anymore; she had been Ilse's age when she did that. There had been fire in her body. *That Ilse*, she thought, *there is passion there, something ambiguous.* Then Frau Zimmerl closed the drapes, for she was tired, and it was so very quiet in the apartment.

5

March 1912

I lse was sure that when she and Annette bicycled to school, their ribbons fluttering, their laughter resounding through Luitpoldstrasse, their skirts swept up by the wind, bystanders remarked "What fine looking girls!"

Though neighbors complained of their speed, they only slowed down close to home. Their sweaty school uniforms revealed the curvature of their breasts; Ilse's lively eyes surveyed the ordinary world with a bold look that said, "See how beautiful I am." In their home they would not be scolded for such fast bicycling, there was love and affection, but not a great deal of discipline. Certainly Frau Zimmerl, so near and dear since Ilse was born, would not complain.

For years the two sisters had their favorite jokes, especially teasing Frau Zimmerl because she so neatly, but slowly, folded the linen, seemingly caressing it. There would be hushed whispers as they prepared school work. In some ways they adored her, but teasing Frau Zimmerl was something they shared. They were excited when they began pen and chalk drawings in their school.

"I'm grateful that this year your school has an art teacher, all those years I took you to the Pinakothek will now be more meaningful," Hedwig said. She took them to purchase their supplies, the school would supply paint, but the girls were to buy different colors of ink, crumbling charcoal, and sharpening knives. Ilse touched her materials gingerly, she could hardly wait to use them.

"The studio visits are at night, and I don't want to go to artists' workshops. I will practice piano then," Annette said.

"We're only going to Schwabing, it's quite grand and exciting. It's a class on proportions, there won't be nude models, you see," Ilse said.

Hedwig was serious, "Would that bother you, if they were naked?"

"I don't know, it would break a taboo I suppose," Ilse said. "But they promised there would not be."

Ilse and her mother were kindred spirits when it came to art. Together they went to museums, the Pinakothek, the Glyptothek; they visited artists in studios. Ilse loved to listen to her mother, so brilliant, as she pointed out features of classical Greek statues or Renaissance paintings. She inspired Ilse when she explained contemporary art, describing the path breaking use of color, as in Franz Marc's recent painting, *Blue Horses*.

"You're so creative, Mama, why didn't you study painting?"

"Why you know, I was the daughter of Westphalian farmers; we did not study like you do. We were well to do, but we were the only Jewish family in our village, anyway, so we only had an elementary education. But I have a good eye, I recognize beauty when I see it. It's your inheritance from my father; he had a sense of artistry though he was a farmer. As soon as he met Moshe, he knew he would succeed. Moshe would court me and I would walk away. My father, may his memory be a blessing, said, 'He's a promising young man, don't be a foolish girl marrying a farmer, this young man will go far. Now for nearly thirty years your father and I have been together and every year has been a gift. The printing press he created, publishing beautiful books, is our legacy to you."

At home Ilse would weasel information about printing processes, woodcuts and engravings. "You aren't planning to open your own press, are you?" Walther laughed, good naturedly.

Strange as her questions were, the family was impressed with Ilse's keen interest in color processing, overprinting and typefaces. When they weren't talking politics or workers' strikes, Moshe and Walther explained different techniques to her, praising her initiative in reading about Japanese and Chinese wood blocks.

Hedwig had decided not to send any of her children to the private Jewish school. As she had never had a chance to study beyond the first classes, she wanted them to have every opportunity to learn German history and literature in the public schools.

Since they attended the girls' public school, the Ehrenkrantz sisters and other Jewish girls were excused from Christian religious studies held early in the morning. At that hour they went to study with a cantor in his apartment.

During school museum trips, the girls' class would pick a work of art and spend nearly an hour looking at it and talking about it. The Catholic girls spoke about St. Francis as they admired Giotto, while Ilse told them about gesso, tempera and fresco techniques.

Voracious in her interest in art, Ilse impressed her art teacher. After she skillfully copied one of Dürer's passion drawings, her art teacher said, "You're so pretty, such a nice girl. I would like to nurture you, improve your talent. Tomorrow," the art teacher continued, "why don't you join the religion class?"

Late in the afternoon, when the sisters returned home, the smell of bleach and soap pervaded the apartment. It was the smell of washing that was so familiar, so comfortable. It meant their school uniforms would be fresh and clean for the next day. Hedwig would be home, and hold their hands or warmly hug them. As Ilse tried to enjoy the familiar sense of comfort, she was restless, she kept wondering about the art teacher starting her on a new path and what choices she had to make. She was on needles when her mother massaged her back.

As they did their homework, Ilse confided to Annette, "Sometimes I wish we went to the Jewish school. I wish we were not different! I feel so much pressure to decide who I am, I struggle to believe. The Christian girls are our age. They take dancing lessons and learn French, just like we do. Yet for one hour a day they learn that we are different. We learn that we are different. Chosen for something. If we are the people of the covenant, what are they? They don't just think our religion is different, they think we are set apart, a wholly different community."

"Shh," Annette said, "they are learning about Jesus. It doesn't concern us. Just let it be."

"You don't know anything about it."

The next day, pedaling ahead her sister, Ilse shouted back, "You go to the cantor, tell him I have the grippe. I am going to the religion class. I want God to enlighten my heart; I want faith, perhaps faith in Jesus as Savior and Redeemer, as Messiah. I want to understand the religion which inspires artists so powerfully."

Nervously she rubbed her lips until they were raw, feeling guilty and ashamed in front of her sister. Wavering and confused, she had begun this habit of rubbing her lips, causing them to bleed.

"Stop it," Annette caught up to Ilse and hissed, "stop it, stop." This time, Annette took Ilse's bicycle handle and Ilse did not bleed, she was prevented from joining the religion class, and she went with Annette. She did not bleed over the cantor's desk and books. That day in the cantor's apartment, Ilse was composed, smiling, only a few dark spots on her lips. It would be her last day there.

As usual on weekdays, Annette, Ilse and sometimes Leon had their dinner with Frau Zimmerl. A sturdy well-polished and functional tea caddy was placed outside Hedwig's bedroom, as she ate two hours later when Moshe returned home. Hedwig wouldn't have dinner without her husband. Walther, who spent his evenings with friends, rarely ate at home. Those friends, it was suspected, included Leah, a young Orthodox woman, but this was still speculation.

Now the familiar, the easy ways, changed for the sisters. As they bicycled back from school or did school work they frowned or quarreled. The subject of the quarrel was hidden from Frau Zimmerl. Annette refused to confide, and since the three of them were often together during meals, there was a hovering unpleasantness, a withering of appetites during meals.

Later in the parlor, Annette said loudly, so that Hedwig would hear, "You don't have to paint halos, you know."

Ilse was furious. "I'm copying a Botticelli painting as an assignment. You're not in that class although you could have been. I'm copying this painting to get a feel for it. You aren't objecting to the radiant dead figure. It's the halo, a Christian symbol that offends you because you believe the resurrection miracle is impossible."

Hedwig came over and they turned toward her. "Why are you bickering? What's the painting?"

"It's the *Lamentation over the Dead Christ*. I wouldn't leave the halos out intentionally. That would be dishonest."

Ilse held out her copy, and Hedwig smiled, "Why, Ilse your strokes are so assured. Though you aren't quite adept at oil yet. I love your pencil drawings though, your handling is so controlled. Annette, open yourself up to the techniques, Ilse can show you how. You are the best musician in the family, let her be the artist."

Ilse thought it was Annette's resistance that made her drawing so mediocre. She was sure her mother thought so, too. But Annette did not give her away completely, she did not tell Hedwig that Ilse had crossed the taboo, drawing her own sketches of Jesus, of Jesus crucified, of his suffering, of the lamentation.

Hedwig continued, "Annette you are musically gifted, Perhaps Claude should come more often. I'm as proud of your playing and singing as I am of Ilse's drawing. Soon you will both be married, love each other while you are home. Don't seek out quarrels. One day your father and I will no longer be here, so you children must support each other."

Frau Zimmerl, gentle and docile, might have taken issue with Ilse's copying of Christian paintings but Hedwig expected her children to succeed in the arts. She was a loving and tranquil mother; she shrugged at worries that might have dogged a hovering mother. She was pleased with her family and her lovely home, and it was primarily her love for her husband that informed her behavior. She waited each night to be close to him, to listen to his daily troubles, soothe his cares, kiss him passionately, close their bedroom door and be intimate. She had space in her heart for her children and she repeatedly encouraged their creativity, but was easy going with them.

Ilse felt free to mingle with the Christian girls and to attend the religion class. She didn't care if the art teacher nurtured her because she was pretty or because she was talented, or perhaps both, for she was accepted in the group.

Now in the cantor's class Annette was a pariah.

"If you sit near me, I will move," said one fat girl with coarse braided hair, who dominated the group.

"Don't mind them, Annette," said Dorothea Liebermann, Max's daughter, a loyal friend to the Ehrenkrantz girls. "They want to force you to tell your parents that Ilse is on a dangerous path."

Annette shook her head. "They don't believe that."

Until now, they had been a warm, tight-knit family, even idealized by others, and Annette would not hurt her parents, disclosing such evil. She did not know what to make of Ilse's behavior and wished it would stop.

She was tortured by insults from the girls in the cantor's class, as they returned to school. As they walked quickly to avoid her, Annette stepped badly and bent over.

"Go ahead," she said to the girls, "I'm going to faint."

"I'll stay with you," Dorothea said.

Annette was pale, collapsing in the school courtyard.

Ilse rushed out and tried to hold Annette's elbow as Annette heaved. "Leave me be, I sprained my ankle, that's all."

"Dear sister, I apologize." The girls, the teachers listened as Ilse apologized, and took Annette's elbow, only to be pushed away.

Ilse said, "She must be in terrible pain," but no one believed her. In variations this scene would now be repeated in school and at home, Annette would be dizzy or retch, until Ilse apologized. Yet even as she apologized Ilse continued to hurt Annette. Christian art was everywhere in Munich with its beautiful baroque churches, it too was Ilse's heritage. Without realizing it, Ilse was influenced by her friends in her behavior and taste. She visited the churches to admire the high Baroque architecture. She was drawn to the sculptures of the evangelists and the painting around the altar in the Theatine church. She walked around the back of the altar in the Frauenkirche, to see the stained glass windows as the light illuminated them.

Now the sisters were cold, cold as ice, to each other. Annette said, "When school is over, I hope never to see you again." She held her body distant, impassive.

Ilse searched her heart, she never wanted to hurt her sister, her family, she wanted to understand about redemption, about the Messiah. Her family believed the Messiah would come, and they believed, as she had prayed daily, that the Lord is One. Was Jesus that Messiah? God would enlighten her. Nervously, she rubbed her lips until they were raw and bled, feeling guilty, ashamed and confused.

In the family, discussions raged about the new conscription proposed by a certain Colonel Ludendorff. Walther managed the family business, and an increased conscription might include him. Worries about the printing press and imminent workers' strikes absorbed both Moshe and Walther. Posters were plastered on the kiosks, with either conservative or socialist messages. Leon, the frail brother, still beardless, was preoccupied with issues of social justice, with the KPD, voicing his contempt for the Prussian Junkers and their militarism. Annette might have confided in Leon, as he was a couple of years older, but he was always either leaving for the beer garden or heading to political meetings.

"The Center Party has no platform," Walther said, "so we have to vote for the SPD now."

Leon squirmed, agitated in his chair, "That political party, the SPD, isn't concerned with the common good, the common man, the poor. They're destroying the future of socialism, and ignoring the forces of history. If the workers' demands aren't met," he stammered, "there will be a proletarian revolution, civil war, executions. "

"Leon," Walther was authoritative, "It's ridiculous to think there will be a social revolution in Europe. Sure, there will be workers' strikes, but they won't have any effect."

Annette was alienated, neither included in raging political discussions nor attached to her sister, who had always been her best friend. Now, Ilse went off to the Pinakothek with the Catholic girls to copy and trace drawings.

6

April 1912

Before Pesach there was much to take care of and both Ilse and Annette, but not together, helped Frau Zimmerl carry vegetables home from the Viktualienmarkt. At Salvatorplatz Ilse went into the private library where gentlemen often read newspapers at a large Gothic table that seated eight. In the alcoves were smaller tables and chairs upholstered in crimson velvet. Locked in glass fronted cases, were books ordered for patrons, mostly collectors' books, first editions, complete sets, and sometimes coin or stamp catalogues. Ilse loved looking in these cases, imagining the first editions she would order, including of course Novalis, Morocco bound, with gold lettering and tassels. She would like many art books, but she would begin, she thought, with Giotto and then collect books on Renaissance artists.

The library was empty this day and Ilse went right over to the collectors' case.

"Herr Fischer, I'm just peeping into the case for a look. I won't breathe hard, I promise, "she told the shop assistant, Gustav Fischer.

"Ethereal Fräulein I am sorry I can't open the case. The books on the top shelf are original Aldine Press books. There's also a complete set of Dickens - another special order, for which the pages haven't yet been cut. Perhaps you would like to see manuscript leaves which we have for sale?" Herr Fischer handled his position with authority, speaking in the most pleasant but forceful way. He had a goatee which was quite funny to Ilse, as he was rather plump.

"Yes," Ilse replied in high spirits, "not illuminated leaves, but I would like a coin book with fine plates. Do you have those?"

"In fact, many of the auction catalogues we carry have plates of coins. Would you be more specific, ancient, medieval, more recent English, French or German coins, what interests you?"

Ilse reached out and clutched his hand. "I want to see ancient Roman coins."

He removed his hand and brought out some enormous boxes and sat with her as she examined coin auction catalogues.

A few minutes before she had not even known such catalogues existed and now she would be buying a perfect gift for Georg. She couldn't wait to surprise him.

"Here Fräulein, this is a wonderful catalogue and the pages are without much foxing, that is, they are not damaged. This is from an auction of the collection of Le Vicomte de Ponton d'Amecourt. You see, the plates were annotated in pencil and a realized price list is bound in. These sheets include Greek and Roman coins. Are you a coin collector?"

Again Ilse put her hand over Herr Fischer's in excitement.

"I'll tell you a secret; I shall be a numismatist's wife."

If Herr Fischer heard, he showed no surprise, it was his job to be discrete and please.

He said, "This is a good catalogue, and the plates are very fine. You must be careful, don't put this near any heat or moisture. Try to give it to your fiancée as soon as possible."

"Thank you, this will be very grand indeed."

Ilse was euphoric when she met Frau Zimmerl at the market.

"Dear, Frau Zimmerl, be happy for me, I'm in such a good mood, I found a wonderful book about coins for my cousin."

Frau Zimmerl was agitated, "This isn't good, keeping up this relationship with your cousin. That necklace you wear has turned your head in the wrong direction."

"Perhaps," Ilse said, "Apollo had no luck and maybe I won't, maybe you're right. Maybe I just imagine Georg's affection for me."

Frau Zimmerl was pale as clay, stammering, "Your parents –how they want to plan your wedding, you need a real beau."

They walked home in silence, carrying packages.

Gingerly Ilse held her new purchase, hoping no damage would happen to the catalogue and that she wouldn't drop the potatoes and carrots.

That evening Ilse read Georg's letters again, kissed the air, and skipped into the parlor to sit by her mother and rub her shoulders. "Mama, I bought a gift for my cousin Georg, I want to show it to you. I have a letter from him inviting me to visit during Pesach." "Yes, I did expect that," Hedwig said. "There's no reason why you shouldn't visit Berlin during Pesach. I'll write to your Aunt Lottie and Leon can travel with you, he's so restless to go to socialist meetings. He'll be thrilled. This confusing situation with your cousin should not go on longer. Either he will propose or you should turn your interest to other young men. Your father and Walther might invite suitors from the synagogue to a Shabbos meal." Ilse rubbed her mouth so that she bled, and ran to clean her face. How much longer would she hide Georg's secret from her family, his intention to become a military officer, and what that required?

At the station, Georg was waiting in a light gray suit with a white bow tie and panama hat. Ilse knew he loved fine clothes, and she touched the fabric of his very debonair suit, how soft and smooth the wool was, and then he offered her his arm.

She could barely wait to give him his gift and handed it to him while they were still walking.

"Look what you've brought me," Georg exclaimed, "but please don't do it again. Leon, tell your sister not to bring me elaborate gifts."

Leon smirked, "I definitely think she should not spend either money or time on you. However now we are in Berlin, I hope you will enjoy these three days. I trust my aunt, so I'm going to leave you without a chaperone."

As soon as they were in Georg's room, Ilse looked through the catalogue with him, they were alone for Georg's parents wanted him to be with Ilse, they, like Moshe and Hedwig, hoped to bring the young couple together.

"Here's a fine silver coin, can you guess whose image it is?" Georg asked.

"It's different, but also in some ways similar to my necklace, is it Apollo?" she asked.

"This particular one is a Greek design; it's quite a rare coin. The Romans were philhellenes and their first coins continued Greek coin styles. Can you see how the designs differ? Look closely for differences, these plates are excellent. This magnificent Greek example is from the fourth century B.C. Look how different the head and curls of Apollo are on this coin from the Roman coin; in this coin he is also facing full front, which is unusual. This coin is from Katane, it's a Sicilian coin, a marvelous coin; look carefully and you can even see the signature of the designer."

Tetradrachm of Katane signed by Herakleidas

"It's amazing. On these ancient coins I notice scratches and fine lines, which must mean they circulated a lot," she said, pleased at her observation.

"Yes, yes that's wonderful that you noticed that. Do you see how some of the coin edges evidence clipping, which means that the coins were debased and the precious metal melted?"

He leaned over her and with his hand over hers, talked about the locks of Apollo's hair, the inscriptions and the different designs. His breath was on the nape of her neck and he bent to kiss her as she turned toward him.

"Now am I to propose? For that's why you came, isn't it?"

"I thought one day you would get on your knees and ask me, but it mustn't be so humorous, so ordinary, like this I must refuse," she said. Ilse looked away, "I will always think of myself as the numismatist's wife, even if we don't marry."

"Oh that is too serious. Now is the time for me to show you real coins of Apollo so you may see how they compare with the plates."

He returned with a tray of coins and picked up a coin with the head of Apollo, helmeted, and held it between his fingers.

"Here's a fine silver coin; there are so many different types." Again he bent over her with the catalogue and the coin.

"Can you see that these are almost the same on the front, but the back has different designs?" She nodded, although she was confused by his cheek on hers.

She put a coin under the microscope and said, "This is the same as another one, they both have a star, why do you have two?"

"You are already thinking like a collector! I want to trade one of them for another coin which is not in my collection. That's how numismatists build a systematic collection. I always try to trade up, to acquire something better, or better for me. It depends too on what my fellow collectors need —the Apollo with a star might complete a set."

Ilse fell into a reverie, she did not see the coins now, but heard horses' hooves, and she did not hear Georg, though she was sure he was talking.

She felt something different than childhood happiness.

"I'm very happy," she said.

"Here's a message for you," Georg said, taking up a pen, and opening a notebook, he wrote:

'Georg loves Ilse'

His dark eyes glowed, his smile was inviting, and his voice was powerfully intimate. It lasted only a moment, then he said, "A marriage has to be complete, to be consummated. You know about that, don't you? You're still a child. There must be a reason – you may not even know – that you brought me Apollo coins, for he loved many women. Did you know that? Women loved him, too, although not Daphne or Cassandra."

"Why are you telling me this? I know about Daphne but not Cassandra. She was cursed, right?"

"Such a clever nymph, you are! Yes I have a reason, Ilse. I love women, I love being around them, and I am always someone's special friend. I don't know that I would change in marriage; I'm pretty restless that way. I would try, though. You're a young girl; you don't understand what I mean, how I might hurt you. I don't mean to sound like a decrepit old man, I know I'm only two years older than you, but my life is different. I am planning to enter the army and women just attach themselves to soldiers. Between men and women there are things you never dreamed of," and he kissed her, a warm, passionate kiss.

The next day they went to the Hoppegarten horse race with his parents. Leon thought it a churlish pleasure, and went to his meetings. Ilse was excited when the horses flew by and Georg held her hand, drawing circles in it. The horses surged forward and then she and Georg had their arms around each other. Between races, they walked around the stables and embraced and kissed surreptitiously. As he kissed her ear, she whispered, "I won't marry anyone else."

7

Late April 1912

After some bustling and nervousness that approached hysteria, Hedwig, Moshe, and Annette were ready to take the hansom cab to the Liebermann home. Walther and Ilse said they would walk. It was a distance, but they enjoyed each other's company. They walked out arm in arm, a picture of sibling tenderness. Leon remained at home, preferring a good book and his favorite chair, by the window looking out on the courtyard. His sisters tried to coax him, saying, "You're so involved in politics. Don't you want to hear the conversation?"

But he rebuffed them. Tonight's party, in honor of Dorothea Liebermann's birthday, was, he said sadly, also a ball, and he would be embarrassed—he was sensitive because of his contorted torso, his deformity from birth.

When the cab stopped at Arcisstrasse 4 Annette almost fell out in excitement. As the servant opened the front door, she was struck by the smell of jasmine and magnolia from the flowered hallway. She felt her mother's smooth, soft, warm hand pressing hers. Bowls of white and yellow daffodils lined the foyer, which looked like an outdoor garden. Annette could hear the tapping of footsteps on the marble floor.

Sam Liebermann welcomed them cordially. "We're really complete tonight! Alas, young lady, you're too young for me, but if I were thirty years younger, I would dance with you! My wife tells me you will play the piano for our guests and persuade them to sing."

Annette wished to reply with something, anything, but she was speechless, dazzled by his garnet and amethyst rings. He escorted them to the music room to show off the grand piano. Silks were rustling as dresses floated by. Already worried, Annette wondered if Herr Liebermann would greet her prettier sister with more ebullience.

However, Sam Liebermann was greeting other guests when Ilse entered with Walther. Ilse gave her coat to a maid, saw Annette and hurried to the piano and played a few notes.

"You should take piano lessons from me," Ilse heard a familiar voice say. "You might even have talent."

She turned around to see Claude approaching with Sara Liebermann. The three exchanged hellos and cheek kisses as Ilse said to Claude, "Why, what are you doing here?" Playfully, she remarked to Sara, "This is hardly his crowd."

Just then, Ilse noticed that Sara had her arm in Claude's, and both had a similar sly look. Were they laughing at her? Had she said something foolish?

Responding to Ilse, Sara said, "I would linger, but I must greet some guests. I hope Director von Rieppel will arrive soon, as my husband is so counting on it. Come Annette, Dorothea was looking for you." With that, Ilse and Claude were left alone.

"It's a party, right?" Claude said. "I usually find my way to parties. How else will I meet important people? Do you suppose students do nothing but study and pray—although many probably do live like that. But I like parties better."

"But how do you know the Liebermanns so well?"

Uncharacteristically evasive, he said, "You introduced us, remember? Are you disappointed to see me? What shall I do if I don't meet lovely young ladies like you?"

"No, not at all disappointed, delighted, really," Ilse said, matching his casual flirtatiousness but still finding his sudden friendship with the Liebermanns strange. After all, Claude was much younger than the Liebermanns. He was twenty-two, the same age as Walther, and he was, well, a scholar. "I hope we'll be sitting near each other at dinner," she said in the same vein.

"Then you can tell me who the fancy people are," Claude joked.

"Oh, so I may be useful, is that it?"

Now serious, Claude said, "Annette promised Sara that she would play an étude, probably one by Czerny."

"Then maybe you can encourage her. Oh, please do; she'll be very happy. Then afterward, please play Schumann's *Toccata*. I do so like it."

"The *Toccata*! Why don't you pick something easy, eh?" He laughed good-naturedly. "Do you want to embarrass me?"

So, they continued, sparring as siblings might, as they strolled to the well-appointed living room. Furniture had been moved to the side so that Japanese art, probably collected by Sam Liebermann during that craze, competed with more traditional German furniture, yet somehow, the effect was pleasing.

Couples were already dancing, and Claude asked Ilse to dance with him. They danced a waltz, a quadrille, and a polka.

Ilse was exuberant; it was her first adult dance party. When her blue satin dress began to reveal perspiration marks, Claude discreetly handed her a handkerchief, and she was thankful. She thought she would never tire of whirling around the room, of dancing with different partners, or of clapping in excitement. Although he was conspicuously dressed in a frock coat instead of tails, Claude was so pleasant—and so handsome— that no one minded. When the musicians paused, he gave Ilse his arm. Then, with great respect, he asked Hedwig to waltz.

The shaggy dog is a fine gentleman, Ilse thought.

Ilse took Hedwig's seat as Annette remarked, "You are quite the dancer, especially with Claude!" She pressed her fingers into Ilse's hand, scratching her sister, and, as if by accident, drawing a few drops of blood.

How cold Annette's hand is, Ilse thought. *Her face is so pale, her gray eyes dull.* Ilse knew her own eyes were shining brilliantly and her cheeks were pink. Wondering who her next dance partner would be, she walked to the periphery of the dance area.

Sam Liebermann anxiously went to the hall to see if von Rieppel had arrived. "Has he come?" he asked.

While some couples continued waltzing, and some men played chess, Hedwig played cards with three friends. Bemused, Hedwig considered her daughters, regarding them over the top of her playing cards. Who would be a success this night? She wanted Annette, so lanky, to be noticed for her piano playing and she hoped Claude would assist her, perhaps even join in a duet; after all, he was her teacher. Still, something about his demeanor told Hedwig he was no more than that; he was not Annette's cavalier. The young man was now dancing with Sara and giving his full attention to the hostess, which was very proper. He wasn't romantically interested in either Annette or Ilse. Ilse, she saw, had no trouble conversing with Claude or other bachelors. When had she developed such confidence?

Hedwig continued with her calculations: Annette's marriage would need to be arranged, for she had no talent for flirting and was a clingy, clumsy girl. She must not become an old maid. Hedwig also had heard that a young man from Hamburg, one of the Neumann sons, was intending to settle in Munich and would be staying at a friend's house in May, after Shavuos. As for Ilse, it was useless to plan for *her* future; Ilse dreamed about Georg and he often wrote her, letters that she hid, Hedwig knew. Ilse resisted any questions about Georg, and his intentions.

Sara was also watching Ilse. She thought her an extraordinary girl. She had seen her alone in the street, so engrossed she would stumble over cobblestones, with a fixed, serious expression that closed in on itself. Sara was challenged by this young, lovely girl who was so unlike the frowning younger sister. Ilse was also unlike Dorothea, Annette's classmate, who meekly obeyed her father.

Sam Liebermann opened the hall door, but the servant gestured. "Not yet."

Temporarily idle, Ilse stood apart, her eyes shining and her face flushed. Sara danced by and, dismissing her partner, suggested to Ilse that they should talk privately. There was a pond with benches in the Liebermanns' garden. After they walked together along the path, admiring tropical-colored begonias, they sat by the pond and removed their velvet gloves, placing their long fingers in the icy water, where by accident they touched. They both burst out laughing at the same time.

When Hedwig, continuing a card game with three friends, saw Ilse turn a corner with Sara, she thought, *Ilse is moving further away from us, sometimes she seems to be in another world.*

In the garden, Sara said, "How curious you are! I noticed you a few weeks ago entering the Frauenkirche—I think you were alone, and you were agitated."

Ilse looked startled, and Sara continued in a conspiratorial tone, "Ah, your secret is safe with me! I very much want to be your friend. You seem so happy here, with your family and friends. Is it wise to live a hidden life and deceive them? If you ever need someone to talk to, you might call on me. I hope you'll accept my friendship. I know I seem overly dramatic, but I have a sense that one day our friendship will be important. You think me superstitious? Well, time will tell."

Ilse wondered why Sara Liebermann, who did not seem like a busybody, would want to interfere in her life—and why she would choose her, so much younger, still a schoolgirl like Dorothea, as a friend.

"My dear Ilse," Sara said, anticipating her, "I want to think of you as another stepdaughter. I hope you'll marry an excellent man. I don't wish to see you ruin your chances."

She is affectionate, Ilse thought. *Perhaps that is the Russian manner.* Sara probably elicited confidences from Claude, too, speaking to him in the same passionate manner. Ilse had no intention of being drawn in—and yet there was magnetism in this very direct intimacy. It was embarrassing and yet flattering.

As the two women re-entered the house, Annette and Claude finished playing a piece for four hands, and the dining room door was opened. Guests found their places as Sara pointed out the seating cards with hand-painted motifs: Ilse was a blue-throated bird in flight; Annette was a clef note. Ilse would have associated scholarly books with Claude, but Sara had drawn a dagger on his card, and placed him between the sisters. *How mysterious, how like Georg's fencing,* Ilse thought.

Herr Liebermann went to the front door each time a guest was announced, but so far, von Rieppel had not arrived.

Sara fussed, helping the older guests to their seats, wanting to ensure that all was properly arranged. More than two years had passed since the widowed Sam had married her, yet she was still learning to run the household. As she turned, the clicking of her heels could be heard on the shiny polished floors.

Some men were still drinking whiskey, and beer and wine were passed around. Before eating, Walther and a small group of Orthodox men said prayers quietly to themselves. Waiters brought the courses in silver bowls, and the conversation veered from disgust at the SPD which was pitting workers against employers, to small talk about the Prince Regent's latest sport, then to the divine Sarah Bernhardt's most recent triumph on the stage.

The servant was opening the front door and Sam Liebermann said, "It must be von Rieppel."

The industrialist finally appeared, apologizing for being held up at a meeting. He had an extraordinary timbre to his voice, and the guests nodded.

"No matter," Sam said. "Glad you are here."

During the main course, Sam Liebermann turned to von Rieppel and said, "Have you visited Serbia? People always underestimate the acuity of the Serbs. I'm looking for business ventures there, and want to suggest partnering with your firm. Last week I was near Sarajevo, seeking business opportunities and then I travelled to a farm in Rogljevo, not too far from Nis. What a marvelous, subtle wine I was served, right from the farmer's own barrels. That's the wine we're drinking now. The farmer is a shrewd businessman and said in German," Herr Liebermann mimicked an exaggerated Slavic accent, "'I can see you are a man of means and a man of taste, Serbian wine is superb, and I grow different wine grapes. If I can export my wine, my wife will have a new dress and my daughter a husband.' Indeed, I may invest in his and other farms, and then contract to sell machinery from your factory to the Serbian farmers. Everyone benefits, including the farmer's freckled daughter."

A stout man with a pince-nez looked at Herr Liebermann with mild scorn. "Really, I cannot see why you waste your time with these small monarchies. Too unstable. You should take my advice, but you are so stubborn. Supply Austria. Do you know General Conrad von Hötzendorf? I am told he is a very learned man, militarizing Austria—"

Von Rieppel interjected, "This political business between Serbia and Austria over Bosnia is most unfortunate. I don't think Austria handled the annexation properly. Luckily the Russians chose not to intervene."[*]

A guest turned inquisitively to von Rieppel. "Do you have any idea how long the new railway in Hungary will stretch? There is wealth to be made there!" To Sam Liebermann he said, "I would supply them with iron if I had contacts there."

"Ah," said Liebermann, "I am willing to gamble some of my wealth on the "penniless" Serbs. They have great aspirations to unite all Serbs; they truly believe they will have a promised land. They are closer to Russia than ever now."

The male guests were engrossed as von Rieppel obliged his host by concurring. "Maybe pan-Slavism is on the rise. Russia accepted the annexation of Bosnia and Herzegovina, but if their patience runs out, Serbia will be a battleground."

As dessert was served, the women conversed with each other, pleased with the evening and with Sara's *salon*—although Ilse overheard one gray-haired matron, meticulously dressed in a lace-topped dress, belittle Sara's accomplishments. "The main course was a success, to her credit. Still she will never match Klara's sense of order. Do you remember how every item was just so in its place? Each porcelain figurine and ivory statue in the perfect spot."

A gentleman with well-oiled hair roguishly interposed, "That does not seem to be why Liebermann married her." Sly looks were exchanged around the table.

Ilse was unexpectedly indignant at the remarks and the looks, but she forgot her anger as Sam Liebermann proposed a toast to his daughter.

---

[*] In 1908 Austria-Hungary annexed Bosnia Herzegovina. Russia, probably too weak militarily, did not intervene.

The youngest member of the Liebermann household beamed as everyone stood to honor her; she had never before been the center of attention. Her uncle Max revealed how hard it had been for her when her mother died and how she had resolved never to leave her father. When he finished, there was not a dry eye in the room.

Sam then pronounced in a booming voice, "Well, I need to tell you that as I have a wonderful wife to care for me—" He was interrupted by scattered applause, "I have urged Dorothea to spend some time this summer with her relatives in Oderberg." With a twinkle in his eyes, he continued, "It so happens there is a very eligible bachelor there, from a family that owns the largest mining enterprise in Silesia. Shall we drink to Dorothea's success winning his heart?"

The guests exclaimed "Hurrah!" in unison as Dorothea blushed beet red, casting her eyes down.

Some of the women gathered around Dorothea, who mutely accepted all the attention. It was, she knew, what her father wanted; but her friend Ilse watched the scene with silent dismay. Sara joined the group, but instead of kissing Dorothea, she took Ilse's hands, saying, "Oh, you'll miss your friend. I hope you'll visit me. I enjoy young visitors."

"We'll surely visit you," Annette interjected, although Sara had ignored her. "Don't be downcast—she's only leaving for a summer."

"Ah, that's not her father's intention," Sara said, turning toward Ilse.

Annette fiercely resented Ilse for dancing with Claude, they were so well paired and lively and seemed so romantic. Now Sara had chosen Ilse as a special friend. Annette felt nauseous and cursed all three of them under her breath. She was so humiliated, she wished she had remained at home with Leon —usually she could get assurance from Dorothea. But Dorothea was surrounded, leaving Annette as the outsider now.

Sara's heels clicked again on the polished floor as she gradually released Ilse's hands and moved toward Dorothea—but at that very moment, she lost her balance on the slick surface and fell down on the floor. Walther and a waiter were closest to her and helped her back to her chair. Everyone was quiet until Sara quickly recovered and said gaily, "Excuse me, I am so clumsy! Please continue."

Indeed, Sara seemed fine, talking to her neighbor, and the meal came to a successful conclusion. Herr von Rieppel expounded on the push of the workers in the steel and pig-iron industries to unionize, and praised the opposition of the industrialists. "Drastic action is necessary," he told the gathering, and everyone concurred. "Fortunately, the Berlin government supports the mill and factory owners; enough has already been done for laborers. You must confront demands for shorter days and better pay decisively. If you waver, all is lost."

When the dessert was finished and the last coffee drunk, Sara could not get up, and Dr. Stern, a guest, took a look at her very swollen ankle. Removing her shoe was impossible in the dining room; Walther, the doctor and Claude helped her up the stairs to her bedroom.

Before Hedwig could stop her, Ilse impulsively headed up the stairs, where Dr. Stern, asking a servant to prepare cold compresses, attended Sara. Ilse sat on the floor and took Sara's hand and kissed it.

"Now I'll be bored," Sara sighed. "Will you come and join me sometimes?"

"You'll soon laugh again, you'll see, even dance."

Looking intensely at Ilse, Sara said, "Perhaps this summer you'll come to our house at Lake Starnberg."

"Well, ladies," the doctor said, "Excuse me, I am going to put a bandage on Frau Liebermann's ankle, and I do not recommend her dancing for several months."

Ilse went over to comfort Herr Liebermann, but he seemed distant, preoccupied. When she put a hand on his shoulder, he said, "My wife shall leave for Starnberg for the summer. I think you'd be a good companion for her, so I'll talk to your father about this. I must finish my conversation with the director."

Within a few minutes he returned to the bedroom, disappointed, as Director von Rieppel and the other guests had already left.

There was nothing to do but go home; Ilse was keeping her family waiting. Walking down the stairs, she heard music, Claude playing the piano. Her family had not meant to linger, yet now, except for Claude, they were the only remaining guests, waiting for her on the porch. Her behavior with Sara baffled Hedwig and galled her sister. Walther stood aside, enjoying the fine evening and smoking a cigar. He said that he intended to make his own way home, perhaps visit Leah, and Ilse joined her family in the hansom cab that was waiting for them.

"It's not appropriate for you to be so friendly with her," Hedwig said as they got into the cab. "We know little about her."

Ilse did not mention Sam Liebermann's suggestion about the summer. Besides, she was absorbed in looking out the window of the cab and listening as Claude continued to play, now a Chopin prelude, its melody permeating the night. Claude was playing with his soul, expressing what she felt.

8

May 1912

"I heard Martin Neumann is in Munich. Is he from the banking family?" Hedwig asked Moshe.

"There's a branch of the family in banking, but I think his father's a merchant, maybe in textiles. They're good people—all their sons finished school, all eight of them, despite many sacrifices. They might be yeshiva boys, an Orthodox family. I'll invite him to lunch with us on Shavuos."

"Yes, that's what I hoped. The rumor is he wants to settle in Munich; perhaps the business in Hamburg can't support such a big family. He might be looking for a business opportunity."

Before the Shavuos holiday began, Hedwig and the cook prepared elaborate dairy dishes, and the house was scrubbed and dusted as if it were Pesach.

"Is he going to eat off the floor?" Ilse asked. "He's old, almost thirty, Mama. Why the fuss?"

Hedwig said, "That doesn't make him old, but mature, which I wish you would be. You're not the only young lady here."

When the men arrived for lunch, Martin was introduced, and Ilse thought, *What's lopsided about his face?* He had a high forehead, snub nose, and curly brown hair. When Ilse came closer, she saw that his eyes were quite nice and hazel, but they were hidden behind thick tortoiseshell glasses. The most arresting thing about him was his height;

he was as tall as Annette—gangly, clumsy Annette. Here was someone Annette could talk to without stooping.

During the meal, Ilse realized what was wrong—the tortoiseshell glasses were barely held in place, slightly askew, and this exaggerated his long face.

The men spoke about the rabbi's lesson during the all-night study session.*

"No one beats our rabbi for drama," Walther said, "bringing the scene of the Israelites at Sinai to life. He stood in front of the congregation and waved his hands as Moses would have done. He asked us to close our eyes and imagine that we were receiving rules and commandments of a religion we forgot, that we were illiterate former slaves. As the rabbi spoke, I felt that I was there with the Israelites, cowering, trembling in fear."

"Yet the Israelites said *naaseh v' nishmah* before receiving the Torah. All that the Lord hath spoken we will do. (KJV Exodus 19:8) Meaning, we will do, we will act, and then later we will understand. They were so ignorant of their past that Judaism would be a revelation," Moshe added.

"A revelation after which they wandered for forty years a distance which would have taken mere days," Leon said slowly, in his halting way.

"It's dangerous to have ideas like yours," Martin said to Leon. "No good comes of questioning God and his love for his people. We are a chosen people with one God and only one. You're a young revolutionary, I am told. You want to help the meek, the wretched, in a new order. Mark my words, such a new order will try to abolish religion." Leon flinched at these words.

"Ah, Leon pushes us to question, to be alert, to notice our surroundings; he's the idealist of the family, that's important," Ilse said vehemently. Where Leon was concerned, Ilse was fierce in word and thought. *Martin rebuking Leon? Leon who was so sensitive, born with a birth defect, crippled as a child. Annette's beau is a callous man, orthodox*

---

* *Tikkun leyl Shavuos*—a Jewish custom of studying all night on the first night of Shavuos. This atones for the Israelites sleeping before receiving revelation at Sinai, as Walther remarks on next page.

or not. I will always shield Leon, it's second nature by now. I am like an
eagle protecting her young.

Martin twisted uncomfortably and whispered to Moshe and Walther,
"I prefer to follow our laws rather than doubt. Too many young idealists
turn from Hashem** and from the love of Torah; it's dangerous and leads
to immorality. Communism, socialism, they aren't our causes, yet for
such causes the most educated Jews abandon the truth of the Torah. In
time they will be our enemy."

Walther jumped in, "Of course your concern is justified, my friend.
For their unbelief, God cursed the generation of Israelites who came out
of Egypt to wander in the desert. We studied about these forty years of
wandering at our desks in yeshiva. Do you remember, Leon, there's also
a Midrash on Psalms connecting the Israelites' sleeping with that curse
of wandering forty years?"

Defusing the tension, Walther began talking about printings of
the Talmud, from the early Soncino and Bomberg editions to more
recent printings in Wilhemsdorf and Berlin. He particularly praised
the Bomberg Talmud for standardizing the text, folio numbers and
commentaries. A weight like a heavy block was lifted from Hedwig, who
feared her hopes for Annette being sabotaged.

Walther wondered how Leah would have reacted to Leon's statement.
Walther and Leah often talked about the future of Jewish Orthodoxy
in Germany— young people were fleeing from the tribe, dreaming of
utopia, a fantasy. Many, like Leon, were drawn to Socialism, to Marxism,
a few to Zionism, but head-on opposition appeared futile. Criticized,
such young Jews would shun traditional religion even faster.

Moshe brought out the booklets for grace after meals. Martin had
dozed off and Leon joked, "He's like the Israelites, who had to be roused
to receive God's commandments—*very appropriate on Shavuos.*" When
they had finished saying the prayers, Walther put a hand on Martin's
shoulder, startling him, and Martin, his cheeks flushed red, groggy,

---

** Pious Jews traditionally refer to God as Hashem ("the Name").

began leading *Birkat Hamazon*⃰ loudly. Abruptly he stopped, realizing everyone else had finished, and recited it to himself.

Hedwig said, "Don't be embarrassed; you were studying all night. Have coffee with us before you leave, Martin."

Annette, wearing a dress colorfully embroidered, brought coffee, cognac, and chocolates to the table. Martin peered at her, but she turned away bashfully, and he thought he might live well with such a modest young woman.

This was a dress for a princess, Moshe thought. Hedwig had planned well. He admired his gifted wife, and her attempt to marry their youngest child, but he was sorry too. *"Annette is so young. Is she ready for marriage, for children?"* Moshe observed the husband-to-be, almost twice Annette's age, and, Moshe thought, a stern man.

"Why, this is a fine idea, Fräulein Annette, to bring us sweets," said Martin. He thought her pleasing, if not as graceful as her older but too high spirited sister. Her smile said *I would make a good wife—I have a beautiful body—we would have lovely children.*

Walther took out a well-thumbed Siddur. "This, my friend, was our first publication in Hebrew, our first direct competition with Vilna's press. Until then, this small firm had only printed Hebrew invitations to *simches*. We borrowed money when we expanded and now our loans are all paid off. Our main business is still German literature, of course, and we have the newest machinery, highly industrialized, employing forty compositors, almost as many as our largest competitor. I'll show you around if you want to visit the printing plant during the week. It's an amazing operation."

The coffee, Annette's modesty and the invitation to the business were sealing a friendship which had almost cratered.

When Martin left, Moshe closed his eyes and twisted the fringes of his *tzizit* in his fingers. He fell into a deep, peaceful sleep and was transported to the old house of study, where as a boy he had pored over the Torah, surrounded by the clattering and murmuring of men with long black coats and fur hats. In a vision, the *melamed* came forward,

---

⃰ *Birkat Hamazon* – grace after meals

close to him, and he smelled his teacher of blessed memory, smelled
tobacco juice and onions as the teacher gestured for him to come closer.
Moshe tried to say something, and tears came to his eyes. Lately the
melamed had appeared often in his dreams, the ancient sage who had
always counseled Moshe, urging him to aspire higher. Things had gone
well for him thanks to the sage's teachings. Every year he dreamt he
went with his family to the melamed's grave in Bialobrzegi, near his
own father's grave.

"When did Rabbenu Asher live?" The melamed tested him in his
dream, after murmuring a blessing. Moshe raced for an answer, as he
had as a boy, anything to keep his teacher from disappearing.

"About 1250, Rabbi."

"Moshe, you were always my best pupil, and you have done deeds of
charity and kindness. See your daughter here, eager for this man, your
guest. You can help fulfill God's covenant, for she is fruitful. She will
bear sons, and they will prosper. They will continue to build your legacy.
Have a care for her, a kind word. In time, perhaps they will love each
other, may it be Hashem's will. Let her approach the bridal canopy and
circle her husband seven times."

That night, Moshe, worried about Annette but also about Ilse, asked
Hedwig her opinion of Martin. Did she think him stern, demanding,
pushy; had Hedwig heard Martin say he had a heart murmur?

"He's a very nice, enterprising man. He's not shy, and he tried to
please Annette. They will be a good match—he's very sure of himself,
of his convictions, and that will be good for her," Hedwig said. "Ilse has
ambition and talent—and she trusts Georg and his promises. She has
already started making fun of Martin, calling him Old Tortoise. She
means no harm—it's just her way, so independent. Annette has no path
of her own and needs a stable, determined partner. Otherwise, she'll
moon over Claude Bertram all summer. Better that she should start
thinking about a husband and children."

9

May 1912

It was Pentecost Monday, a German holiday, and they had an excursion planned. The night before, her cousin Georg, visiting from Berlin and restless, had asked, "Aunt Hedwig, may we go to the countryside tomorrow? There's a fine horse parade at Bad Kötzting."

"Why, of course!" Hedwig replied enthusiastically. "What should young people be doing indoors? Just ride over to the Simons' and invite Martin Neumann, and you should also invite Dorothea," Hedwig added, to no one in particular.

Ilse did a celebratory little dance, while Annette frowned. Georg persuaded Hedwig that he and Walther would be escorts. Ilse first rode over to the Liebermanns' and invited Dorothea, then over to the Simons'.

Returning home, she removed her cape and danced by herself in the foyer. Hedwig called, "Ilse, your hair is wild now from that little dance. It's so mussed! What have you done? Come, let me fix it."

Ilse stretched her hands out to her mother and danced toward her. As Hedwig braided Ilse's hair, she continued, "Martin might not be used to your barbaric behavior, so can you try to be ..."

"I promise modesty. No hair pulling, no spitting. I'll be very prim."

Hedwig ran her fingers along Ilse's cheek and left them there a few moments. "You distract young men. Go exploring with your friend and Georg, and let Annette and Martin enjoy the view from Swan's Inn."

Ilse put her head on her mother's lap and thought to herself, *it's about*

Annette, all this mystery. How very intriguing. Martin is supposed to fall in love with Annette, and I am to keep out of the way. That's why Mama agreed to this trip. What if the Old Tortoise falls asleep again? Walther will arrange a tête-à-tête! Mama has courage, too, risking that Georg and I might be alone, but she wants a decision about our future, she's not sure of him. So she's agreed we travel on a Christian holiday.

On the day of their adventure the little band carried oranges, kosher buns and flasks of tea and hurried to the station. Martin would meet them there. Ilse wore her pendant, the necklace from Georg. Her skin tingled when she pressed it to her chest. She was breathless when they neared the majestic terminal, a hall of iron and glass. People were rushing with valises, carrying children, porters lifting and unloading trunks. Good weather and a spring holiday—the station throbbed with escapees to the country.

"Ilse," Walther said out of concern, "don't daydream, stay near us."

They were at the kiosk, along with half of Munich, when they heard Martin calling out to them—he was hemmed in by crowds, awkward.

Poor soul, Ilse thought, looking at Martin. *He's wearing that same heavy, dark wool suit with the vest he wore to our house. He doesn't know what a country holiday is. Those clothes must be several years old, and his shoes are quite worn too. Frau Zimmerl says he's looking for a very good wife; she's smart, she means a rich dowry.*

"Lucky to have this fine weather," Martin, now extricated from the crowd, was saying as he clasped Walther's hand. Walther and Martin towered over Georg, but Georg had such an athletic appearance, with broad shoulders and muscular arms, that Ilse thought the others seemed unmanly next to him. She noticed how lustrous his hair was.

As they dashed to their train, Martin extended his hand to Annette, and they indeed looked like a happy couple. Annette smiled gratefully, and then he was right behind her, clambering up into the train, trying to stay close to her. Ilse saw his back end, thought *What an oaf,* and then hoisted herself. The train whistle blew, the train sped up and the young men bonded, talking about their stamp and coin collections, while Ilse looked out the compartment window at the crowd and waved until Annette mocked her. "Of course, you think they're all waving back at you."

Once they left the city limits, they rolled past villages and farms with neat houses, and ivy decorating the windows and doorways, in a landscape dotted with steeples. The road was crowded with peasants enjoying the holiday, on horseback, on bicycles, on foot. The young men, in loden green jackets, were wearing lederhosen, and the peasant girls were dressed in dirndls. The peasants were of all ages, some wrinkled, some young and muscular, all moving together, the men wearing red sashes and feathered hunting caps, creating a festive tableau.

Ilse thought how staid their little band looked compared to the colorful peasants. What if they had worn more spectacular clothes? Perhaps she could have worn pants—that would have created a stir.

Annette and Dorothea were whispering secrets, while Walther warned Georg and Martin, "We have to be careful not to let Annette and Ilse pull us in different directions. Lately, they rarely agree."

Walther brought out his volume of Darwin's *On the Origin of Species*, saying it was a difficult read that tested his beliefs, and Martin said, "Good reading. Indeed, his ideas about the origin of life provide very useful topics, especially as an entrée in meeting customers at our warehouse. When I mention Darwin, I get different reactions, and then I know more about the buyer and his beliefs. It usually opens a discussion that leads to a substantial order."

"Did you read Darwin recently?" Walther asked, to make conversation.

"Well, I hear a great deal about him, about some of his more outrageous ideas. I haven't gotten around to reading this book yet."

Ilse tried to say something not too biting. "Surely you don't think your buyers are such baboons?"

Walther quipped, "Martin, be glad Ilse is on good behavior, or we would face a harridan."

Ilse thought it was an extraordinary way to do business, manipulating customers in such a crass manner, such an odd, almost philistine thing to do, perverting important ideas.

"Ilse has a point," Walther said, letting her know that he too thought Martin rather shallow, but also ending the conversation, turning to Martin, "I will lend you my copy when I finish." He wasn't going to ruin Hedwig's plan.

The little band left the train at Regensburg and then split up at Bad Kötzting. Ilse and Dorothea wanted to hike in the woods; Georg and Walther chose a difficult trail on the mountain, while Annette and Martin stayed at the inn, admiring the lake.

In the hills, there was the sweet smell of aconite and conifers. "It's lovely here, looking for wildflowers," Ilse said. "Who would imagine that my reserved cousin, who usually spends his Munich visits at coin auctions, would convince my parents to permit this trip? Why, he's quite appealing when he chooses. My parents think he's charming."

"Really? What do you think?" Dorothea teased. "You're right, though. This is better than doing homework, and now we're lighthearted, having this beautiful hike. We're quite free."

A shaded path eventually led the two friends to an alcove of firs, where they gathered wild strawberries and arranged bouquets of aconite and primulas and searched for a place to eat the strawberries with their oranges. Then they realized they were hardly alone—carousing couples who had wandered away from the center of town were seeking love and pleasure. Ilse had never been in such an embarrassing situation. It overwhelmed her—the bright-green and white dirndls, the jackets set aside on the grass by couples embracing —these were scenes she dreamed about, had been constantly dreaming about since she went with Georg's family to the Hoppegarten race course. Now observing the entwined couples, her body felt strange and hot, as it had then.

The hours passed quickly as she was spellbound by this scene of pure energy and life. True, there was much carousing and kissing on Sundays in Munich's English Garden —the atmosphere was bohemian in Munich, full of young artists, their lovers, their models, young students, and followers, but such intimacy was not seen in public spaces.

Two peasants played the harmonica, and some women sang:

Wenn ich ein Vöglein war
und auch zwei Flüglein hätt,
flög ich zu dir,
weil's aber nicht kann sein,
bleib ich allhier.

If I were a little bird
And also had two little wings,
I would fly to you.
But because that cannot be, I remain just here.**

Ilse and Dorothea knew the melody, and they hummed together
softly. Then they shushed, hoping that none of the couples heard them.
They were afraid that if they moved, some peasants might notice them
and realize they were voyeurs. Ilse wanted to remain rooted to the spot,
because she felt a warmth and sensation through her pores, a strange
stirring. She felt her nipples harden and wished she could press them
against one of those plump farmers. Her knees were pressed together,
almost painfully.

The sunlight waned, and the air was fresh; a soft breeze carried
exciting smells to the two girls, smells of sweat and beer. As the peasant
groups began to move away, Ilse realized she was perspiring so profusely
that her dress was soaked. The couples were quickly vanishing, fulfilled,
happy and laughing now, running to see the horse parade and the
fireworks and drink more beer.

Ilse and Dorothea finally felt they could leave their hiding place, and
they started back, hoping they too might see the parade before catching
the train home. Ilse regained her composure, but as they walked, they
met a pilgrim family praying and singing Christian hymns. Dorothea
tensed, but Ilse felt a sudden exaltation as the family stopped to talk
to them. The family had an air of tranquility; one of the girls looked

_____

** · Translation by David K. Smythe, printed by permission of Lieder.net.

directly at Ilse and asked, "Would you join us as we walk and pray? We are reenacting the walk to Emmaus, retracing our steps."

Dorothea hurried to say, "Oh no, we must catch a train. Thank you."

As the family moved away, Ilse watched them, entranced. They were so graceful; they seemed to be floating. Their song was clear; it was a joyful, happy song, and Ilse stopped to listen. Dorothea was tugging at her. "Strange, they thought we were Christians."

In the town, the band was playing, and crowds were gathering for the whip crack competition. An array of horses, covered in colorful blankets, with yellow and green bonnets, was lined up, the riders wearing the traditional black and red costumes, and the priests in bright red robes. After the competition, the horses circled the crowd before proceeding to the church and Swan's Inn. Ilse knew she was awake, and yet the sound of hooves was exactly like the clopping in her dreams. Georg was walking toward her, and she felt prickling excitement, a peculiar, not unpleasant feeling. Was it because her dress now clung so tightly to her breasts that Georg's eyes fixed on her? She felt there must be something immodest and shameful in her appearance; she worried that in her woolen dress her breasts appeared plump and prominent, her skirt tight. Clearly, Georg was responding to her sensuality. His looks made her blush pink, and awkwardly she fell and cut her knee and felt a fool.

"Let's walk together to the train. We'll try to bandage that knee," he said to her and Dorothea.

The train whistled, and the wind blew in from the steel door as they left Regensburg. The sky was already turning a dark purple, as the train passed a small village, and they heard church bells. Ilse said, half aloud, "Someone has died. The funeral bells are calling the townsfolk to pray for the deceased."

She was sure everyone was asleep, when she felt Georg's hand on hers as he whispered, "May I hold your hand, Ilse?" Time passed. Ilse was not sure how long. Georg held and squeezed her moist hand and then kissed her fingers. He had turned down the wax lights in the compartment and then kissed her on the lips, a long kiss. She thought if the others were not dead, surely they could hear her heart pounding. But everyone else was sleeping. With his other hand, he used his handkerchief to wipe off some beads that had formed on her nose and forehead.

She was afraid to breathe as she sat motionless; she felt her own wetness and was afraid Georg might smell it. He must have been smoking and drinking beer, as she caught the faint scents of both mixed with his masculine smell. She now confused his face with one of the bearded, red-faced farmers—she wanted to squirm and squeal and laugh like the peasant girls who sang of their love. Mixed in was the praying family and their song and the mournful church bell, the disparate sounds reverberating as one melody over and over, in which the bells tolled, pounding in her head.

"Relax," Georg said. He moved her hand to his knee, where she kept it stiffly. He fingered the pendant of the bezeled coin, moving his hands toward her breast.

As the train pulled into Munich Station, Georg moved her hand, ever so slightly toward his groin, looked at her directly, and said teasingly, "Have I not been the best escort? Will you give me a good mark? *Fräulein*, your bouquet, you would not want to forget it, such beautiful wildflowers." When he handed the crushed flowers to her, she realized she had pressed them tightly between her knees.

Getting off the train, her body felt warm, and she forgot Dorothea, her sister, her brother, and Annette's beau, as crowds of people pushed into her. She realized Dorothea was tugging at her sleeve, saying, "Look at Annette, helplessly in love."

Annette was listening intently to Martin, both standing erect, and Ilse caught a few words: "The Fugger compound ... the banking dynasty." It occurred to her that Annette would marry Old Tortoise and that the business arrangements, the dowry, Martin joining the printing press, would be settled before Martin returned to Hamburg,

She was sorry to be distracted—for where was Georg? She looked around anxiously; she wanted to kiss him again. She now realized that the rocking sensation of the train, that pounding, was very arousing. She was perspiring again— under her arms and under the soles of her feet, and there he was, saying, "What a delicious day. We'll have many more, won't we?"

Dorothea was again tugging at her as Ilse turned to Georg and whispered in his ear, "Yes, we will."

10

June 1912

S ara was on crutches, Dorothea was in Silesia, and Herr Liebermann insisted that Ilse join his wife at Lake Starnberg. On Rosenbuschstrasse, arrangements were being made for Annette's wedding. This included bringing Martin Neumann into the business as a future partner. Ilse was only too glad to escape, to let Annette be the center of attention, for the wedding would be in January.

Ilse admired the Liebermann villa, with its simple exterior and symmetry. Built in the English style, it appeared modest at first glance, but the interior was elegant, with a rosewood staircase, carved doors, and elaborate fireplaces. Ilse's bedroom, up a flight of stairs, had a balcony with a fine view of the lake. Ilse and a housemaid shared the upstairs. The master bedroom was on the ground floor, near a guest room. Every morning, Ilse rushed out to the balcony and blessed her private sanctuary. Beyond the lake, she had a spectacular view of the Alps. In the afternoons, she watched the sailboats, white shimmering against deep blue. Hadn't Sara predicted they would become close? Now she was plucked from her family, glad to avoid Old Tortoise's almost daily presence. Ilse wished for only beautiful summer days and calm nights in Starnberg.

At first, the two women, one still young, the other half her age, tentatively felt their way into a friendship, tiptoeing around neutral topics. They spoke about the heat, the wind, the cloudless sky. They read novels together; they compared vilified heroines to lady killers, and agreed that the heroines were beguiling and their husbands and lovers callous.

"Why don't male novelists criminalize adulterous men? In most cases, men just get a slap on the wrist. They don't despair or seem lost. Instead they are treated as conquerors," Ilse said.

"Time is the great villain of love affairs," Sara said wisely. "Look at Anna and Vronsky, day after day together, with no way to escape. Time is their nemesis. Poor Anna who could light up a room with her smile— fate was unkind to her. But time can also be cruel to married couples. I wonder how Sam and I would get along if we were always together. He would surely get fed up with my toilette, my spending hours brushing and putting up my hair, coiffures with pins and combs. It would drive him insane. He would probably wade into the lake there and not return."

Ilse said, "Sara, you are laughing at me. Surely you agree that Effi is a different heroine. Married too early?"

Sara was mournful, "Perhaps to a husband too old, or both. The real crime in the stories is the treatment of children, isn't it? They're the victims."

On Friday, Sam Liebermann arrived by train with other businessmen joining their families. Sara, still on crutches, was up at dawn; Ilse could hear her in the garden. Looking out her window, she saw Sara collecting dahlias and hydrangeas. By the time Ilse descended, bushy plants had appeared on the window bench, and flowers were in bowls on the table. As they prepared to meet Sam at the station, Sara dressed in lavender, with her hat, her shoes, her bag all matching. She was hobbling in the dining room, stopping to smell the flowers.

Ilse was troubled but simply said, "You are a different person today, all dolled up. And your hair is down—it's so long!"

Sara said, "After all, I see my husband only on weekends; I want the time together to be special. He surprises me each time with some charming gift, and I do my best to please him, wearing colors he likes and jewelry he has given me."

Ilse remembered the older gentleman as controlling the dinner conversation, but also as a beaming, exuberant host. She anticipated seeing the husband and wife embrace, as her parents frequently did. The train arrived; families crowded the small station at Starnberg with a happy, festive air, and the men joined their families. Sam Liebermann was finishing a conversation with her father's friend, Ezra, both men holding shiny canes, and he approached Sara with a half-hearted embrace, barely acknowledging Ilse's presence. He was clearly absorbed in his own thoughts, while Ezra, heavyset, went to greet his own family. With difficulty balancing her crutches, Sara kissed her husband.

On the way to the villa, Herr Liebermann talked incessantly, and Sara listened dutifully. Ilse felt quite alone, looking at their backs, resisting the urge to scream. It was astounding how Sara had suddenly changed. The friend she adored had disappeared and been quashed, taking on the persona of the simpering, obedient wife. When they arrived at the house, Ilse sat outside on a bench, and she heard Sara—thumping on her crutches—join her husband in the master suite, pretending that she needed to unpack his small case. Ilse walked down the road to the beautiful lake, trying to understand why Sara felt so inferior to her husband. She hoped her friend would come and join her, and sat by the beach house until dusk.

At dinner, Sam Liebermann was remarkably voluble and friendly. They had beer and fish soup, and he spoke of neighbors in Munich. Then he heatedly mentioned that in Munich, the talk was about the Balkans and about degenerate elements there. He tried to explain about the Balkan League but became confused, saying darkly that he had heard about this secret group from his Serbian associates. Confidentially he told them—although Ilse hardly understood, ignorant of the people he spoke about—that Pašić was not a man to be trusted. Yet he had personally received assurances from Pašić that Serbia, where his cash was tied up, would not enter into hostilities with Bulgaria.

Ilse had hoped she would be able to pique his curiosity and seem a part of the family, but she was unable to find a topic of conversation as he continued to dominate the evening talking about Serbia, the Balkan League, Bulgaria, Sazonov, on and on. Sara was listening intently, her eyes gleaming, an adoring look on her face. Later, after a few more beers, he nodded off in an armchair. As the maid cleared the table, Sara and Ilse whispered, but after a few minutes, they started speaking more naturally.

Feeling comfortable with Sara again, Ilse ventured, "Did my presence inhibit a romantic hug or kiss? I expected your husband would lift you up and twirl you around!"

"And he would have, but his mind is preoccupied. His life is work, work, work."

Ilse wanted to believe Sara, for she thought Sam was not affectionate. He had been hearty in Munich, but now he was cold to Sara and to her. He was roused when he spoke about Serbia or matters linked to his finances. Sara had to be passive, behave like a worshipful disciple, a child hoping for a reward, for him to feel vigorous. There wasn't any conversation between them. It was only necessary for Sara to be well dressed and have a wide smile.

"Do you understand this? Is it something serious that will hurt you financially?" Ilse asked Sara.

"I know who the players are; I sometimes read the Russian paper. Before we left Munich, all seemed fine; something must have changed quickly. If there had been trouble this morning, Sam would have stayed in Munich," Sara replied.

"Are you happy?" Ilse blurted out.

"Why, silly," Sara said, "marriage is not a game. There is dependence, you know. My husband depends on me for understanding and comfort, and I, of course, depend on him to provide for me. It seems a fair exchange. Can't you see I live the life of a princess?"

Suddenly she said to Ilse, "When I came to Germany, there was a famine in Berdichev. Starving villagers stole bread from the children of others, and especially from poor Jewish children. Now, when I watch children play, I try to forget this. Jews never had a better life than here in Germany; Sam made it possible for me." In a voice barely a whisper, she added, "The poor children— be glad you have never seen hunger, and mothers watching their children die."

"Oh, Sara, I will always protect you!"

"Why, you are just a girl—but how very sweet that is!" Sara exclaimed, her grim reverie broken. "When people say things like that, my sixth sense takes control, so perhaps a time will come, though I can't imagine how or why, when I may turn to you. Who knows? But now we are brooding. I will ask the maid to help Sam, and we will all have a good sleep. Good night, my dear." Sara gently kissed Ilse and gave her a light with which to go upstairs. With that dim light, Ilse saw that Sara did not go toward the master suite but disappeared into the guest room.

As she fell asleep, Ilse missed the voices of her parents, missed the familiar smells of home, and seeing the tea caddy which announced to the whole world that later, in their bedroom, Hedwig and Moshe would delight in their great love.

When she came down for breakfast the next morning, Ilse noticed her friend absentmindedly pouring coffee, buttering bread, and replacing it on the wrong tray, visibly anxious.

"Sam has just gone out to see one of his acquaintances, who is well informed," Sara told her. "He's absorbed in his work, unable to relax, and he fears his Balkan venture is in trouble. This crisis will surely pass."

Ilse, quick and sure in her opinions as a young person, thought that Sam Liebermann was a greedy old man who wanted a beautiful wife, success in a venture in a violent area, the inducement being delicious wine.

"Let's sit outside," suggested Sara, and the housemaid brought them coffee, but unlike the previous days, when they sang or told stories, this morning they were quiet. It probably was not long, but it seemed hours until Sam Liebermann returned, hastily coming upon them.

"Sorry, ladies, I must return to Munich."

Sara sweetly folded herself in his arms and he hugged her, quickly, then handed her one of her crutches, saying:

"I am sorry, my dear, but luckily you have your friend here to entertain you. Fräulein Ehrenkrantz, I wish we had more time to talk. You seem such a delightful young woman. I'm glad you joined us. The situation in the Balkans is alarming. I must not lose the value of the goods I shipped there."

"Are you traveling to Belgrade?" Sara asked anxiously.

"I hope not. I need to be closer to a reliable phone and receive telegrams. I'm very sorry." Hurriedly, he called the maid to help him pack.

The two women picnicked later that day; the weather was fair, and they walked along the beach in the afternoon, meeting other women from Munich. These gatherings turned into parties, with wine, beer and cheese. Some of the younger women sang; one had a flute, and the music led to dancing and hilarity. A few of the women had scandalous news to tell, rumors from Munich about liaisons; older women with younger men and older men with young mistresses. Ilse could see that her presence restrained them, but she could not help blushing red when the women laughed about some of the more outrageous trysts.

They made tennis dates for the week, and then groups of women returned to their homes, but Ilse and Sara stayed behind, since no one was waiting for Sara.

Sara said, "You see how rare good marriages are! But I know one thing: my Sam is monogamous. Marry well. I wish for you all that you want. What about that young Frenchman?" she asked teasingly.

"What?" Ilse was startled. "Oh, Annette's teacher, of course he's very likable." Then Ilse dismissed the thought; Claude didn't interest her. Instead she said, "Ah, you don't know my cousin Georg. He's so handsome, such a great horseman, and he's different. He's so special, extraordinary, ambitious, I could go on and on…Claude is like the lovers in the novels, a ladykiller."

Sam did not return the following weekend or the one after that. Sara's ankle healed, and in the hot sun, they walked down to the lake, wading in and swimming, and then sitting close to each other until their swimsuits dried. They discovered vistas for drawings or watercolors; a calm lake with sailboats brightly colored was a perfect tableaux. They painted the blue-green shades of the water, the pastel sunsets.

Ilse borrowed a neighbor's horse and galloped along the water's edge. She thought of Georg and how, as youngsters, they used to ride together at Norderney, a memory of childhood. Georg would hold the reins for her when she rode a skittish mare. When they got back safely, their parents would embrace them and dry their sweaty bodies with towels.

At the beach one day, in the sultry heat, Sara said, "I hope to meet this wonderful cousin Georg."

"I do so like him, but it's hard to describe," Ilse said. "When we were toddlers, our families would meet in the summer at Norderney. We would play in the sand, run in the waves, at first only with Walther. I have sweet memories of the warm sand, our small hands touching in silly games, and the water splashing around us. Later, our families formed competitive tennis teams. In the evenings, Georg and I occasionally cheated at cards, but we were usually caught, and Walther and Annette humiliated us. We told outrageous lies, convinced we were very sly, and every so often we were believed, forcing everyone into a distraught search for a cat or a favorite book. Once when we were really young, we smeared the walls with jelly. We were inseparable, sometimes letting Leon join our gang.

"We were children; we talked about marriage as children do. We came to believe in it. I love the word *betrothed*, don't you? It's such an evocative word. It sounds divine. A few months ago, I went with Georg's family to the Hoppegarten racecourse, and with some prompting, I put money down on Ariel, a wonderful thoroughbred, elegant and sleek. I watched through binoculars with my heart thumping during the last stretch. She was winning, she was amazing, flying toward the finish line—Ariel was first. I imagined Georg riding her, so splendid, both man and beast sweat-streaked with powerful chests."

"You're stirring me up to love him too."

"Oh, he is my *bashert*, my intended! There, as Shakespeare wrote, is the rub: Georg is so ambitious and so determined to succeed in the German army. In Berlin, his parents are assimilated; he's their only son, and they support his decisions. You know, some rabbis in Berlin have pushed the door open, wide enough for Georg to believe he can convert, be a Prussian officer, and still be accepted in the Jewish community."

Sara was clever enough not to show disbelief. "That's why I saw you at the Franciscan church? I knew it was a special moment. You were so focused; I waved and called to you. Can you persuade him not to convert? I suppose that's what you mean."

"No. In fact, I don't want to persuade him. I want him to have a brilliant career. But I want to marry him, and my parents will oppose such a marriage."

"You seem so complete and happy at home, it's incredible. You know, Sam and I are not traditional Jews; we don't observe the rules and rituals, but the idea of forsaking Judaism would jolt even Sam. Think of the pain and scorn your father's family endured. In my village in Russia, I saw children dying of hunger. I saw old Jews brutally beaten in the street, women run over by wagons, synagogues desecrated." Sara, sitting there in her wet bathing suit, her braid reaching her waist, was weeping.

Ilse put her arms around her friend and said, "There must be a devil in me; something inner propels me. My school friends are Christian. I kneel with them at school. I dream about conversion, that a new life will begin."

"A life that would destroy your parents, what kind of life is that? Think about what this means to your family. Marry Georg, enjoy your lusty youth, have children. From what you told me, Georg hasn't really changed his identity, he just made a pragmatic choice. You can love God with all your heart, pray and fast. But hold off on conversion, on leaving your Jewish community. Otherwise, you will burden your marriage with such enormous guilt that it won't survive. Your parents love you. Your mother fears losing you— I saw that at our party. She was disturbed by your attachment to me; your parents will die in grief if you take such a step."

Tears glistened in Sara's eyes. She said, "Not many years ago in Russia, Jewish babies were kidnapped and baptized and their mothers left bereft. Mothers wept and begged magistrates to return their babies, their pleas denied. Sometimes if they degraded themselves, yielded their bodies, they would get their babies back. There are Jews in Russia, members of the Bund, the intellectuals, who became *apikorsim*, they could not bear so much suffering. But you are not doomed or fated to become a heretic.

"Do you remember that I drew you as a bird? You will be crushed like a little bird. Your song muted. You must be struggling so on such a serious matter. And afraid at the same time. If you want to confide in me, I will be glad to listen; I won't bring it up if you don't."

Enough had been said.

Sara did not want to cause a distance between her and her young friend. She did not want to repeat what Ilse surely had heard from her parents. Ilse was relieved; Sara's face and body revealed no horror, as Ilse had feared. Sara was distressed, but there was no withering coldness or sudden revulsion. Sara became even more attached to Ilse. Perhaps she thought it her mission to save her friend. She tried to imagine how Ilse had reached this point—such a clever and lively girl. What dark corridor had she entered?

In the following weeks, they continued to paint, take long walks, speak of tragic heroines, chatter idly. *More contention and discord would be too hard*, Sara thought.

"When you marry Georg," Sara said a few days later, "don't let him become a man who knows only work, work, work. Sam is a good man, but he is unable to relax. After Klara died, he focused on his business; it became his 'son.' Now he cannot tear himself away. He has tried; he comes out to Starnberg but almost immediately finds a reason to return to Munich."

"Aren't you lonely, then?" Ilse asked. She thought to add, "Without any children?" but repressed the question.

"Ah, but I have you, as a younger sister, you see. And Dorothea. I am not lonely. I love to read and paint, just as you do. I especially enjoy young people and would like to meet your cousin Georg."

Ilse thought that loneliness explained Sara's apparent interest in Claude, for Sara would sometimes mention him, twice getting goosebumps. Ilse didn't think much about this, probably a cold breeze affected Sara, perhaps Sara hadn't healed completely.

As her friendship with Sara grew, Ilse had ceased thinking of Sara as Dorothea's stepmother. Sara had a girlish impetuousness that resembled her own. She was not preoccupied with philanthropy, with the Centralverein, for one thing. At Ilse's home, there was much talk of Jewish communal activities; it was part of daily life. Sara never mentioned these. Perhaps she occasionally joined the women in Munich who did good deeds, visiting widows and orphans. Yet she seemed more like a young girl herself, not quite ready to care for others.

The two enjoyed the beauty of the lake and dreamed of a wonderful future and long-lasting friendship. They sat in the sun, lazing in the Liebermanns' bathhouse. They painted portraits of each other and they were well matched in tennis games and at cards.

"How sad I am that this summer is ending," Ilse said on one of her last mornings in Starnberg.

"My darling girl, so am I," Sara said and kissed Ilse gently on the lips.

Then Sara teased Ilse about kissing Georg and asked how Ilse liked being kissed on the lips.

Ilse said, "Really, Sara, it's wonderful. I want Georg to kiss me and hold me tightly. He's so manly. Like other officers, he's grown a mustache. Listen, when we were at Hoppegarten, it was hot— rivulets of sweat streamed down the horses' bodies. When Georg and I went to collect my winnings, no one watched us, and well," Ilse stopped and brushed her hand across her lips. "Georg, well, he threw off his jacket, unbuttoned his shirt to cool off and, giddy from the race, we kissed, his chest bared. I kept thinking that's the chest of the man I love, my lover. It happened so quickly …"

"Oh, you are so ready to be married!" Sara said.

Hugging at the station, Ilse said, "Whatever happens, I will take your advice. I know you are smarter than I am about marriage. You've managed to live independently, just as you wish, and please your husband. It will be complicated to marry Georg if I don't convert, but we will find a way. God knows what is in my heart. You are right; I cannot face my parents' sorrow. I am not hard enough for that."

The driver took her suitcases and hatbox to the platform, and then the carriage whisked Sara back to the villa, as Ilse,—her heart full of love—watched her friend drive away.

11

August 1912

The sun cast a bright-yellow light on Starnberg, which Ilse knew she would remember all winter. *Home*, she thought with joy. She anticipated her parents' loving embraces, their gentleness, her pleasure hearing the rise and fall of their voices. She was now a mature young woman, and yet she had missed her family, like a child. The bohemian flair of the house on the lake entranced her. In Starnberg, the house was festive in color—violets, oranges, greens—yet it was not her home. Now she was looking forward to the staid apartment with its somber Biedermeier furnishings and heavy drapes.

After she was seated in the train, Ilse took her book out, but within a few pages, she was daydreaming, thinking back on Norderney. Leon had been so contorted; he dragged one foot and endured painful operations. Ilse was only seven then, and his suffering was impressed upon her memory. Through winter and spring, Leon would look forward to summers in Norderney, often speaking about the coming summer. Each year, they put on family skits, and Hedwig painted scenes for a stage setting. Annette and Ilse helped sew costumes, and Leon memorized long speeches. By the time Leon was ten, there was a slight improvement in his walking, though he still limped, but he was happy because his step-cousin Georg promised him an orange kite.

Then came the very last summer the family was together. Georg would hardly play with Leon. He told Walther he wanted to be with the

other boys, the Kissingens, Baumgartens, and Cohens who bowled* or
sailed. He refused to play in a skit with girls. He now read Karl May's
Westerns, not stories about Talmudic rabbis. Although Leon walked
better, to Georg he appeared more disfigured. Georg didn't want to be
Leon's kiting teacher although Leon was handling the kite well—yet
heartlessly, Georg said "Leon I wish you well, but I can't be your best
friend. Forgive me. You have other friends, I am sure."

Ilse looked up when the train reached Munich, still recalling how
Leon loved his handsome cousin Georg. She understood Georg's need
to belong, to be like his peers, to conform. Only, she wished he had not
hurt Leon, who never forgave him. Leon, who had always been different,
had no empathy for Georg.

It was late afternoon and humid when Ilse reached the apartment
and removed her hatpins in front of the gilt mirror, and was startled when
her father joined her in the hall. Was he home especially to welcome her?
He embraced her warmly, was unusually solicitous, and covered her head
with his enormous hands, reciting:

"I say of the Lord, my refuge and stronghold,
My God in whom I trust,
That He will save you from the fowler's trap,
From the destructive plague.
He will cover you with His pinions,
You will find refuge under His wings;
His fidelity is an encircling shield.
You need not fear the terror by night,
Or the arrow that flies by day." (Psalm 91, KJV)

This was not a traveler's prayer, but a psalm. Her father seemed
tortured by a perceived danger, warding off demons. She felt the same
deep love for him that was inspired every Friday night when he recited

---

* boßeln – propelling a ball, usually in street, still a popular game in north
Germany.

Kiddush, when he poured the wine, when he gave her the honor of distributing the challah.

"Papa, I was not in danger," she said, as extraordinary possibilities filled her head. *Had something happened to a steamer in Starnberg? Had trains collided?* "Why are you crying?"

Her father loomed over her and clutched her by the hand, pulling her into the dining room. "Your mother and I will explain everything."

Anticipating company because Mr. Ehrenkrantz was home early, Frau Zimmerl had arranged yellow chrysanthemums in a pretty vase, and Ilse stared at them for a hint of why her father now had tears in his eyes.

It was strange to be sitting at the dining table when it was not Shabbos, something that was hardly ever done; the gloom was broken only by the chrysanthemums. Frau Zimmerl had outdone herself.

Ilse thought of Frau Zimmerl, diminutive and fat, rushing to the florist when she heard Mr. Ehrenkrantz was coming home and ordering the cook about in the kitchen. Yet, it was no time to be amused, for Hedwig was telling her to sit down. Moshe sat at the head of the table, his head bent. Leon, still thin, still pale, was perched at the end of his chair, his feet swinging anxiously. In the shadow, by the door, Annette stood, a pillar of anger.

Unbidden, Ilse's fingers lightly brushed her lips. What possessed her father, her mother and sister, and why was Leon so agitated, he too focusing on the flowers? Then she noticed a letter on the table. She reached for the letter; she knew that florid cursive—it was from her aunt Lottie, and she now understood that the crisis was about Georg.

"Your cousin," Moshe said, with shaking hands, "your cousin is an apikoros, becoming an apostate," he blurted out.

This was the ugly truth—in her parents' eyes the idyllic romance she envisioned in Starnberg, would be disgusting, horrid. Ilse was startled and frightened for her father; veins protruded from his neck.

"Cholera," Moshe cursed and repeated, "cholera," and with that curse, he threw up his hands.[**]

Sara had been right. Ilse's parents would never understand her—they had no idea of her genuine longing for God. Those Giotto copies over her bed were so foreign to them that they dismissed their significance. It was the same with her reading of the New Testament and St. Teresa of Avila. It was so alien to them that they gave it no thought.

"Georg?" She uttered— she had known this moment would come.

She and Georg had often written to each other about the implications their conversion might have for their families.

She read the letter aloud. "'We hope you are well and your sweet children also. Werther and I have been working on a new edition of the Winckelmann letters and the first volume—'"

"Nonsense, nonsense!" Moshe shouted, shuffling the pages. "Here, here!"

Frightened, Ilse hesitated. She felt a strong, friendly hand on her shoulder; it was Walther, who had entered the room and stood beside her.

Ilse read: "'Georg was accepted into the military academy. He has developed confidence and has been more settled lately, become a more caring son. Here in Berlin, the military presence is everywhere, and he has long wanted to be part of it—not as a cadet, but as an officer. He says it is a grand thing to be in the Prussian army, where only the best become officers. He is a favorite of the ambitious Colonel Ludendorff, who is already making quite a name for himself, and Georg accompanies him to staff meetings and even to military headquarters. No doubt you have read about this officer, Erich Ludendorff, who took Georg under his wing. After the election, Ludendorff's star dimmed, but Georg says he's the best military strategist in Prussia.

"'Georg is passionate about the army and hopes he will have a chance to prove himself, which in Berlin is possible only for Protestants. Georg is indeed converting. We wept when he told us the news, but his baptism, under the circumstances, is not such a surprise. It is to be this Sunday,

---

[**] · Cholera was greatly feared in Poland in the early 1900s, so that the expression was considered to have the power of a curse.

a small affair with just a few of his fellow cadets. We have written to all the family members …"

Moshe snorted, took the letter, and continued reading. "Like your Ilse, he has a dogged streak and is determined to succeed, so we hope you wish him well. Werther and I support Georg in his ambition and will fund his commission, which is still far off. We hope that he will be welcome in your midst. During their holidays, we will invite Ilse and Annette to visit us, as in prior years. In any case, Georg will be at the academy. Since he and Ilse are good friends, he will probably write his own letter to her."

"My darling girl," Hedwig said in the pause that followed, "this must be difficult for you, and we cannot make it easier. We didn't know how Georg was leading you on. Pretending that he would marry you, while he was planning conversion. Pretending a romance that he knows must surely end now. It's our fault—we also failed." With icy calm, her mother concluded, "You would be dead to us if you continue pursuing Georg." Ilse had never heard her mother speak in such a controlled, angry way.

"Mama, I never pursued Georg," Ilse said, and at least that was true.

Annette, who had largely gone unnoticed, screamed, a sound midway between a screech and a howl, a sound of pain. Her eyes bulged, and she gurgled as if vomiting. Ilse sat numbed, aghast. She would have escaped if she could have.

Annette was feverish, as if she only half knew where she was, and seethed. "You are planning to convert. Tell the truth; confess it. Martin says we must flee from you, never to see your diabolical face again."

Still shaking, Annette continued, "You don't see how evil you are. You think you can get away with following a false religion and never tell anyone."

In that room, in which no voice had ever been raised, the walls echoed "convert, abomination, diabolical."

"What did she say?" Moshe asked, quavering. "Do you understand what she said?" He turned to his wife. Hedwig was stunned, abjectly crumpling the letter.

"A fool would forsake our faith to ram a stirrup. But it won't happen in my home. A whole day," Moshe raged, "I manage to forget the misery in Poland, how the *goyim* spat on us, like Haman. Simple people, our gentile neighbors, stole our goods and tormented us when the Russian soldiers massacred Jews. We must drown out the names of Hamans and obliterate the names of heretics. Do you understand?*** It's not possible that my child would leave our community."

Ilse hesitated but said, "I am interested in the church. How could I not be? It's all around us. Everywhere there are beautiful churches, such glorious architecture. The creative genius that built these churches is godlike. Our lives revolve around feast days; they are already part of our lives."

Bursting into tears, her father said, "You're deluded, my child. These outward images have nothing to do with us. Many of the images and symbols were created to oppress and offend the Jewish people, to offend you and me, do you understand? You will break off any plans you and Georg may have made." Ilse's heart hammered. "Promise me you will not become one of them. So sorry, so sorry, for tears," Moshe said, his voice breaking, as he tried to stop weeping.

Hedwig added, "Your father is right. In Berlin, the new movements, so liberal, are misguided. My dear daughter, their way is not ours."

Walther had been quiet, and now that his father's anger subsided a little, he said, "We must be strong as a family. We don't accept intermarriage, and almost worse, mumarim. Perhaps, Ilse, we can parse this curse on heretics. So you understand better what you are doing. I want you to sit with me now while we review the Mishnah."

Thin, pale Leon, perched at the end of his chair, turned their alarm into movement, his feet nervously beating the air. "If you ask me," said Leon, not looking at anyone, "Georg has done the Jewish people a favor." He was clenching his fists, jumping out of his chair, going for his coat, going out, going for beer; he did not want to stay another moment, he said resolutely.

*** Haman, villain in the <u>Book of Esther</u>. Conflated with all oppressors of Jews. See *Reckless Rites* by Elliott Horowitz, chapter, "The Eternal Haman."

"I am not thinking of converting," Ilse said decisively. "Still there are matters of belief that touch me, and I must ponder them, think them through. I need time to consider them. Suffering, love, and faith are connected. I need to understand what is in my heart. Jews and Gentiles are connected."

Walther brought the Mishnah to the table and read the section relating to the curse on *minim*, heretics. "May I give my interpretation of this text, in case it's not evident to you, Ilse. Consider the time when the sages dealt with heresy and the curse was formulated. The Temple had been destroyed, and some observant Jews, who still kept *mitzvoth*, were accepting Jesus as the Messiah. Many of these 'heretics' didn't even think they were splitting away from their heritage, from their community. It was a devastating time, a time of controversy and pain for the sages. Even then the Mishnah makes it clear good and pious Jews were led astray. Indeed, a generation later, Rabbi Elisha ben Abuyah, a great sage, became Judaism's most famous heretic. Even after his apostasy, he remained a brilliant scholar and Rabbi Meir studied with him. But Georg is a confused young man, and we must not consider him an outcast. Instead, we must help him return to Judaism of his own free will. Only false prophets are beyond redemption, but Georg will be redeemed. You will see, Ilse, he will not remain a mumar. That isn't possible; with your help he will have a change of heart. Rabbi Elisha may not have gone the route of teshuvah, but I know Georg will. Judaism is kind to the Jew who does teshuvah**** and we will all help you, both of you, just as Rabbi Meir tried to help Elisha, whose tears saved him."

Moshe said, "My comfort has been in the Torah and my family, how can these be different? Your mother and I dedicated our lives to this faith, have we failed?" His anger was assuaged by his son's words. Walther was an incisive interpreter of the Mishnah, and since his courting of Leah, he devoted himself to study every evening. Walther moved closer to Moshe and they both wished they had been able to educate Georg.

"He doesn't spite Judaism," Moshe said. "He doesn't even know what

---

**** Teshuvah - repentance

Judaism is. I failed you, my own daughter, if you even consider leaving the faith, the community, which I love. I thought my love for Judaism would be contagious. You're not ready yet to make a decision and I'm convinced you will make the right one. If you leave our faith, it is a nail in my coffin. I won't forbid you from writing to Georg, you are my child, and I won't do that."

"Dear," Hedwig said, "Georg is a misguided young man. Why, it's only a few months since he visited here. Did he mention this to you, or is this a hasty decision? You are wrong, if you think you can be in two worlds, the Jewish and Christian one. We have the challenge- here and now- of not abandoning any Jew. We won't congratulate young Georg, but we can visit Berlin, and their family may join us at holidays," her voice trembled.

In school the next day, Ilse wrote to Georg:

My dear Georg,

How unexpectedly everything turns. You have been my friend from childhood, and we swore to tell each other secrets and to convert at the same time. I find I cannot do it now. Your parents have accepted your decision, but my parents cannot. I never saw my father cry before, and should I be the cause of such tears? I'm not so brave, though I was the one who cheered you on. Also Annette made a scene; her suitor Martin is a fanatic and she has turned against me.

It's not so easy in Munich, the Jewish population is tiny and even intermarriage is unusual. I heard gossip in Starnberg, and almost every sin is admissible but not conversion. Don't think badly of me, at least during these years our trust in each other brought us closer, hasn't it? Also, I kept your secret and I know you kept mine. My conviction hasn't changed, and maybe that is just as sinful and evil.

You must write me of your daily routine. Do you march for hours? Do you drill for parades?

Will you write and tell me whether you feel inwardly different during your religious instruction? Do you feel like a better person now, as if you experienced a death and rebirth? I am sure when I convert it will be like that—everything will taste better, sounds will be clearer. I will be in an ecstatic space. I will be charitable and kind, which I am not now. Every day I fail to be good, to be charitable.

Please do not leave out any details; I want to share your experience. I shall imagine you with two other soldiers, sitting in a cold, gray room with a young pastor, and now you are discussing religion. Or maybe you are standing, or pacing anxiously because of your uncertainties. You are asking why God would need to create three out of one, why the Trinity? It seems pagan to you, and the young pastor with twinkling eyes hands you another text and then another. He reminds you of original sin and redemption. Why is church doctrine so cruel as to condemn Jews to remain outside the fold? Is it the Church that divided the two beliefs, or conversely, Judaism that condemned Christianity? For surely the two religions complement each other. Jesus understood that.*

Who indeed is an apostate? The Bible doesn't say anything about conversions.

Even the pagans believed in the soul.

Mein Soldat, read my letter with charity!

We have spoken several times about marriage, having a family of our own. I don't know if you still feel the same way. All these years you asked me to wait, you were not sure of yourself. Your mother writes that you now have confidence, have you been able to make a decision about our future?

I do not know when my parents will allow us to see each other, they are in some shock.

I wish you were close to me, encouraging me; you are the only person I can trust now. I will try to explain my feelings to my mother, you have my heart. It will perhaps break without you – without your kisses.

Yet I remind myself that you have never seriously proposed. You have even been devious, continuing the game we played as children.

---

* For certain terms and ideas, I used an unpublished Introduction (available on the web) to a forthcoming book, <u>Bastards and Believers: Jewish Converts and Conversion from the Bible to the Present,</u> eds. Theodor Dunkelgrün and Pawel Maciejko. This Introduction may be found on *Academia.edu.*

When this storm blows over, as it must sometime, I would like to be with you.

Joyfully, Ilse

She sealed the letter three different ways and asked one of her school friends to post it.

12

From Munich to Berlin

Throughout her childhood, Ilse wanted to feel carried away by something, and transcendence and marrying Georg were intertwined in her hopes and dreams. With her schooling over, Ilse was adrift. She had the leisure to read the books she wanted and go to the museums, often with her mother. Yet a spark was missing.

She spent too much time questioning herself. Was it really impossible to hold two beliefs? Jews had been beaten and marginalized and killed by Christians, she knew this. How dark Jewish history was, full of suffering. And yet, she saw the sky above and small miracles happened every day. She didn't live in that world of pain. Why couldn't she accept the Torah and Talmud as her guide the way her family did? *I must be hollow inside*, she thought. *Diseased.* Each day she hoped to wake up and be the version of Ilse that her family desired but over time her father's and brother's protests and pleas were barely audible.

Months passed and in early 1913 Annette's wedding preparations organized the Ehrenkrantz family. The day came and went. What a wedding, everyone said. What fine clothes. What fine foods. The Ehrenkrantz and Neumann men—including Martin's seven brothers— were in top hats, of course, and the wives so finely dressed. Now the Ehrenkrantz and Neumann families were connected. Who would be there for Ilse? Dorothea had married the rich Silesian industrialist and hardly came to Munich now, especially as she was pregnant. Ilse visited with her school friends but they shared a Catholic upbringing and Ilse understood that their lives did not contain her. Ilse only occasionally saw Claude when she and Sara went riding, making their way across the fields. Even her time with Sara seemed reduced for reasons that were not clear. She became Walther and Leon's protégé, Walther would sit with her over the Mishnah and Leah lent her books about important Jewish heroines. Leon brought home weighty tomes on Communism, and she did try, not very appreciatively, to read a novel by Chernyshevsky. With Walther she read from *Pirkei Avot*, as he pointed out important passages, for her, such as,

"*Run to pursue a minor mitzvah, and flee from a transgression. For a mitzvah brings another mitzvah, and a transgression brings another transgression. For the reward of a mitzvah is a mitzvah, and the reward of transgression is transgression.*" It was inspiring to think that way, that one good deed leads to a better deed, a good thought to a better one.

Walther treated her with respect and love. She had never paid much attention in the cantor's class, which involved reading the Bible chronologically and when she left it, the class was up to Kings I. At home she had often heard about the schools of Rabbi Akiva and Rabbi Shammai, but she hadn't really paid that much attention. Walther helped her read the Talmud—to understand how these schools differed. During breaks in her studies, Leah would take Ilse to the *mikveh,* the ritual bath and they became good friends. Walther taught her the cantillation of Biblical tropes, the *taamim,* which she liked to practice until she became proficient.

She was questioning, worrying in her belief. Was it impossible to hold two faiths? Jewish history was dark and full of suffering. Suffering mostly at the hands of Christians. Ilse felt she wasn't welcomed to the *Wandervogel,* the youth group of her Catholic friends, when she joined them for long walks. What was it that so eluded her, the chasm between these two faiths?

She struggled with the Apostle Paul's letters. She would have liked to have been at the Mount of the Beatitudes, to have been a disciple

---

** Quoted from Chabad.org

who heard Jesus preaching. She was with Jesus and his disciples at Gethsemane. She spent hours reading and re-reading the Book of Revelation. Without instruction in the Christian faith, how could she know her heart? For that she would have to leave Munich.

Tranquility came to her when she received Georg's letters. Perhaps it was a reckless distraction but she waited anxiously for them. Now a lieutenant, Georg wrote to her regularly. She imagined him writing by a warm lamp, sharing his adventures and ambition and desires.

March 17, 1913
Dearest Ilse,

I was so happy to get your letter and read about your Jewish studies, dearest rebbetzin. Be pious, devout, what you will, as long as we can be together.

Today a group of us traveled to an inn near Brandenburg for an evening meal. I have written you about Moritz, such a talker. Well within fifteen minutes he had so charmed our young waitress, a very pretty girl, that she brought us double and triple portions of everything. We were stuffed and had drunk ourselves silly so that when the owner came with the bill, we couldn't get up to pay and leave. Some soldiers were nauseous and vomited and so we had to sleep there until the morning. Our bill, with lodging the whole group, was huge. We hardly had that much money and I had to get everyone to empty their pockets. I expected to put this responsibility on Moritz, but that Lothario disappeared with the waitress and we did not see him again until we got back to barracks. He will certainly get some young girl pregnant. I had to gather all of our funds and tell a good story to the owner that hinged entirely on duty and honor and love for our country. It was settled but I came away with a moral—that we should avoid that restaurant when you come to Berlin. When are you coming?

I am tossing restlessly in bed; I want to see you, feel you and hug you.

May 10, 1913
Dear Ilse,

I am waiting for you in Berlin, waiting every day to embrace you, hold you close. I want to be your happiness and joy. I cannot get away now because of my training and perhaps, in truth because in Munich I fear your father's stern disapproving look. And still, my heart is full of hope and love that we may be together. I feel empty without you. I know you are struggling because you don't want to hurt your parents. But what about your happiness? And what about mine? Family is important but we should have faith in ourselves. I know that if you have the courage, all will be well. Come to Berlin. My parents will find a suitable accommodation, do not worry.

In time your parents will realize you are happy and forgive what they consider a trespass now.

At the academy, our company marched yesterday for three hours until our feet burned in our shoes. We are constantly on the move, eyes straight ahead, then on the perimeter, on guard against things that we can't even imagine. Finally, today, we were allowed to hunt small game in Schlaubetal. We set out with dogs and reached Bremsdorfer Mühle, which has a small farm. A sow was sunning herself, with her young buried in the mud. One of the soldiers, Hans, became enchanted with one of the piglets, and paid the mill owner to sell the piglet to him. Hans had his pinscher hunting with us, put the dog's leash on the piglet, christened him Caro, then dragged him along, as the pinscher barked and the pig grunted all the way. When we arrived back in Berlin, Hans refused to give up his adored piglet and so we marched through the crowds in the Zoological Garden area with the noisy pig and the barking dog! We care for all things German, even our swine. You can imagine we were quite a sensation for the children in the area. In the end, Hans determined he would donate the piglet to the zoo, and then he had to pay the warden to take it. to be continued

May 11, 1913 continuation

I feel disquiet about a venture I have just begun. I want to know more about the mill and how it functions. The young men have goals and dreams;

but they won't work at the mill all their lives as their fathers did. They worry as newer machines are being introduced by the mill owner.

Their stories of village life, the marriages, romances, hard work, struggles, these need to be preserved. Soon industry will overtake our German farmers and mill workers and I am writing down their stories. In short, I am their chronicler. I created a small journal with a friend, we're Ovid and Polybius, and we will print stories for fellow soldiers. If it is read and becomes popular, we will convert it to a subscription journal. We're calling it Undertones.

Before drill I visit Bremsdorfer Mühle, watch the laborers leaving for the mill, this is about five in the morning; children still sleep at that hour. By the time I leave for the academy the schoolhouse has opened and daily life goes on pretty much as it did centuries ago.

In the evenings, I go to the pub and ask silly questions, but I find the men willing to talk, especially a fellow about my age, Carsten.

He was born in the village and knows stories from his grandfather's time; His grandfather was the village elder, apparently a tyrannical 'ruler'. People feared him for years, but he successfully negotiated with the mill owner, so his iron rule was tolerated. There was enough to eat and drink and the mill owner was kind and generous.

Yet in 1817 the village fell on hard times, as did the country, and during the famine, people died of typhus and starvation, there was no grain in the village, no potatoes in the field. A rebellion formed in the village, but no one accused the elder. People didn't know that all Europe was suffering after the wars, they only knew about their own village and some other nearby villages. Cärsten's grandfather, convinced he bore the guilt of the community, lay down and refused to eat, his bones pierced his skin, his face became spectral and gasping, he died. He died for his village. At first the villagers did not understand his act, but the following month the flowers bloomed, the fields flourished and grain was plentiful. Young women gave birth to healthy babies.

I want to connect this story to the idea of sacrifice in many religions. Even to the idea of human sacrifice, so powerful in ancient times. It can be found in the sacrifice of Isaac, the sacrifice of Jesus, and other ritual sacrifices which, in Judaism and Christianity, lead to redemption. Symbolically, the village elder was a Christ figure, willingly sacrificing himself. It may not be melodious, but I hope when you receive your copy, for I will send you one, you will approve.

Love, Your Georg

Ilse read with rapt attention. She realized something that had been dormant in her heart, that he was a dreamer, in many ways like her, but also like her father. He was emotional and creative and a risk taker. She felt an ache for him, was willing to risk everything for happiness with him. She thought of the open display of intimacy between her parents, so unlike other families and she longed for that type of life. She was sure she and Georg would be such a couple.

Georg was magical fields, conversations, curiosity, and poetry. He was a dream like blue horses and things still unrecognizable to her. She read his words and felt a need to be with him that only intensified with each letter. Georg burned with curiosity and through his words, she saw colors and lines and paintings and affirmation. She also envisioned shadowy implications for her already challenged life with her family and she didn't quite know what to do.

January 15, 1914
My dearest Georg,

What you have shared about civil marriage and new laws is a relief. It would be easier if we might marry in front of a judge and step back for one moment from the form of wedding I have always understood. You as a Lutheran, odd— and I would still be Jewish. I can't imagine you baptized without me, but so it is.

I miss you terribly, but I know we will be together soon when it is easier for me to take flight. Maybe if I took the final leap, it would not be so shocking to everyone, for so much is happening here: Annette gave birth to a baby boy two weeks ago, just circumcised and named Jakob, and the business keeps Papa busy. Mama worries about Leon's revolutionary activities, his ideas would destroy our comfortable lives. Why would he harbor such ideas? So many fearful and complicated issues now—like Papa I believe in Germany, and I know you do too. Yet there are thoughtful people like Leon who believe our way of life is doomed. We read in the paper about terrible workers' revolts in Russia, where the farmers are so poor.

My friend Sara Liebermann frets about her husband's business in Serbia.

January 16
Continuation

I fell asleep before finishing the letter last night.

Then today I received my copy of Ovid's Undertones. *I was absorbed by the history of the Herero peoples of Africa, which might be forgotten if not for your archives. We never learned anything thorny in school, although we knew there was an African continent, we never saw any pictures of Herero life. It's important that Germans atone for this crime against the poor shepherds. We aren't alone; England and France are also killing African peoples. I don't understand that cruelty. Aren't we well off here, why do we kill Africans, why should we compete with England and France? I will pray that you will never have to kill and murder other men, and that you will be a success in the community without violence.*

What a great thing you are doing keeping alive the memory of these shepherds.

I wish I might be with you, writing beside you, perhaps assembling the research notes. I knew you were an encyclopedia!!

Lots of hugs,
Your Ilse

While this correspondence continued, and intensified, Moshe and Hedwig invited Jewish friends from the community for the Shabbos meal, especially those with eligible sons. Menachem Dresser quickly became Ilse's favorite from this parade, quite possibly for the flower always peeking out from his jacket pocket.

Menachem was a young scientist, fascinated by the natural world, by the laws of gravity, by laws yet to be mathematically proven. His faith was in science—he was an agnostic who still went to the synagogue out of consideration for his father. Walther discussed Darwin with Menachem, when he visited at the Ehrenkrantzes. Sometimes Ilse and Menachem went for walks or enjoyed the museum. He was tall and dark, and together they looked a stunning couple, and she took some comfort in this. The two families were already congratulating each other even though there was nothing definite between the young people. He had a passion, Ilse recognized that, admired it, but could not share in it. To be ambivalent about God was something she could not reconcile with her spiritual convictions.

Tenuously he talked about marriage because that was expected, and it reminded her of the years when Georg had flirted, dangling marriage. When Menachem asked what she wanted in her life, if she could imagine a life with him—his voice squeaked, betraying his fear. Everyone knew that Menachem wanted to marry, he wanted a family. Her mother could barely hide her grin. But Ilse felt a coldness, she did not believe Menachem desired her, how could an agnostic live with a wife who obsessed about religion? How could she imagine living with a rationalist, skeptical of revelation?

"Do you collect coins?" she asked him one day.

"No I collect stamps. I have some very unusual ones, are you interested to see them?"

Ilse said, "Yes, I'd like to see your collection."

He collected stamps from all over the world, he told her, not just rarities. He wasn't specializing in any one country, and he showed her his albums. There were many classifications, stamps from Europe, the British colonies, America.

When he spoke about his stamps she longed to hear him say they were "amazing" "incredible", or "wonderful". She waited to learn what stamps revealed about their society. But his explanations were dull. She smiled then at her own certainty created out of a state of uncertainty. Menachem was right in front of her but no embrace from Menachem could keep her from loving Georg.

At home, Ilse retreated to her room and clutched her Apollo pendant. The weight felt substantial to her, an anchor, and the small rubies around the bezel, which her friends admired, were like Georg's passionate words, beacons that led her back to him despite time and distance and obstacles.

Time was passing without Georg's mouth on hers, she despaired. She dreamed of him, and hugged him in those dreams. She sensed Georg's indefatigable energy pulling them together but knew that his life was also about maneuvers and artillery, and he was busy with his writing, while her time was spent with a heart thudding in her body, waiting for something numinous.

And so she was walking on yet another day in the English Garden with Menachem by her side, breathing hard with an expression of desire on his face, while she noted the warm weather and blooms around them. Menachem had been accepted as a Privatdozent at the University of Göttingen, and while he would not have any salary there, he would assist Professor David Hilbert, incorporating special relativity courses, promulgated by a certain young physicist named Einstein, into his department. For Menachem, this would be a grand opportunity. He would be leaving Munich soon and he wanted her to join him.

"Ilse, marry me, come with me," before she could respond, he kissed her tightly. She felt his teeth against her lips, painful and abrupt. She had not noticed before how small his mouth was. She did not feel the blood rush with his lips on hers. She felt instead something close to revulsion and in that moment, Menachem sensed her rejection. The antipathy of that kiss was not fulfillment but rather conclusion.

They continued walking, without speaking. Ilse knew then what she had to do. She needed to risk everything and find love and warmth with Georg. It was her only chance.

For the Passover Seder in 1914 Hedwig and Moshe invited the Dresser family. There were twenty two people at the Seder table, not including baby Jakob. By the time the Dressers left it was two o'clock in the morning but the following day the Ehrenkrantz and Dresser families were at the synagogue early. Ilse and Menachem had not spoken privately since he left for the university and, as he walked her home from synagogue, she noticed something different about him. He no longer looked at her with desire and instead of walking calmly by her side, he was spry and lively.

"Ilse, I met someone in Göttingen, a mathematician, so rare among German women. I know it sounds crazy but I discovered that very thing you spoke of, that invisible spell and I love her totally. We plan to marry soon and I want her to be the mother of my children. I hope you'll congratulate me."

Menachem had found what Ilse desired and as she held his hand warmly, she cultivated a growing confidence that she knew what she must do.

Ilse waited for an evening when Hedwig was alone and joined her in the parlor.

"Mama, there is no one here for me. Menachem is engaged, to a mathematician. We had little in common, he's a genius I am sure, but we're on different planes. I wish you knew Georg as I do; he's like Papa in all the good ways. He's a dreamer; did you know he is publishing a small journal? He has turned himself into a chronicler of cultures and peoples that are endangered. I have brought you a copy of his journal, it's only four pages, but it's important work.

There's more too, he's wonderfully masculine in his uniform, yet he has a soft side like Papa. I would like to travel to Berlin, not only do I need to get away from here, but I can also help him with his journal."

Hedwig cupped the back of Ilse's head.

"Please Mama, I must do this."

Hedwig was frustrated by such rebellion. In her heart, she also sorrowed for Ilse, whose dream might be bittersweet for them all. Ilse would be caught between two worlds. Yet if Georg was warm and kind like Moshe, the couple would be happy. Certainly Ilse would respect a husband who was inventive and creative. Hedwig took the journal into her bedroom and began to read about Germany's colonial empire in

Africa. She had never thought about that part of the world, or the people living there, and she was engrossed.

Both Georg's writing and his insight were remarkable—he displayed a different side in his writing, a humane side, while probing and analyzing Germany's colonial protectorates. Moshe too was impressed with the four page journal, which reminded him so much of his own beginnings.

A week later, Ilse left home with her suitcases and a hatbox, pressing her pendant tight against her chest.

When Georg met her in Berlin, it was as if she had stepped into a painting that he had created for them. He stood there waiting and receptive, the sky above them limitless as he reached for her hand and pulled it to his lips. He never took his eyes from hers even with the noise of the crowds around them. The impulse to kiss him was overwhelming but she waited for him to pull her to him. He leaned in and kissed her quickly right there in the train station.

Days passed and each day they had their little adventures in and around the city, walking, reading and feasting. In the lush Brandenburg forest, they held hands and had picnics that stretched across entire afternoons. When they entered Café des Westens in Kufürstendamm, Ilse saw how other women envied her. Was this life really possible? Could she feel this womanly and actually be the same girl that she had been?

The sounds and rhythms of his language became familiar to her. He filled her head with images and songs and wisdom. She was impressed by his writing. He made the farfetched believable and the mundane a kaleidoscope of wondrous excitement. Each day together was the very thing that she had sought. When May brought balmy weather, they went boating on the lake at Weissensee. Under the light blue sky, and enveloped in a breeze, Ilse felt nearly hypnotized. She saw Georg unbuttoning his shirt. He let go of the oar and without warning jumped straight into the water, sending the boat into a rock that nearly tipped Ilse in as well. Ilse looked over the side to see Georg's face concentrated and determined.

"Let's get married at the registry, Ilse. And let's do it soon." He splashed her face lightly with the cold water. "Jump in if you agree."

He was meant to be her husband. She felt a cool splash against her face and she jumped in, fully dressed.

Georg smiled as he pulled her to him and kissed her there. He held her palm to his lips and whispered, "I will always take care of you, you know that. I will always be with you. Even now, I will make sure with that bundle of clothes, you don't drown."

They embraced in the water, beside the boat, floating on the love they generated between them despite the weight of her clothes pulling them down. People clapped all around them and hearing this, Ilse clapped her hands together as well for this was real, after all and not a dream. "Yes, I know," she said.

Georg brought her to a soldier friend's apartment, supposedly for their clothes to dry, yet his hand was so tight over hers as he led her up the stairs that she was not surprised when he undressed her. He kissed her shoulders and breasts and her inner thighs. He loved her in the end, he said, and in the beginning, and also in the forever. "I have been waiting for so long," he told her, and putting his lips to her ears, he kissed her there too as they made love for the first time.

By the time they returned to the Eddingses apartment, it was night. Lottie, ever hopeful and diligent, waited up for them, stalking them in the hallway at the first creak of the door. Ilse saw her standing there, the doting and devoted mother and thought of Hedwig in her chair beside her father. That was the life she had left and this was her new life.

"I suppose this means we are arranging a wedding," Lottie said gleefully, kissing Ilse and hugging Georg. It was clear to Ilse, that Lottie was truly happy for them. Lottie had faith that her brother Moshe, with his soft heart, would relent in time, and the families would be reconciled. Ilse, as a Jewish woman, would marry a converted Georg so all was not lost for the children as Moshe would see it. "All will be well, Ilse," Lottie offered. "No need to worry. Now it's time to celebrate."

"I would like to call Mama, and share the news," Ilse said, perching on a chair with an anxious exhale.

"Of course," Lottie said, in the calm, kind voice that never cut anyone short.

The telephone wasn't perfect, the operator too slow, but finally Ilse got through to Munich and she cried, "Mama, I have news to tell you. I hope you and Papa will accept it - for Georg and I will have a civil marriage. In June, Mama. Here in Berlin, it will be easier. It will only be close family. Will you please come, Mama?"

13

June - July 1914

On June 29, 1914, Ilse and Georg were wed. For their honeymoon, Georg suggested Venice. As a child, he had been there with his parents, and he was resolved to return to that bewitching city of gold and stone. Their wedding had been a small affair—her parents and Walther would not come; Annette was pregnant again, almost in her fifth month, it seemed. Only Leon was there representing her family. Her mother sent a letter—*I love you so much*, she wrote.

"We thank God it was not a Jew who killed the Archduke," Leon whispered to her at the wedding, a day after the stupendous news from Belgrade that Austria's heir to the throne was assassinated.

Georg rowed standing in the Venetian style, his light white sweater lifted by breezes and the boat swept into the lagoon. Ilse watched the swirling water, the exquisite azure-blue water of the lagoon, admiring the orbit of Georg's hands, his muscular frame, his wavy russet hair freed from cockades, insignia, and emblems.

"In Berlin, they would not recognize you," she said gaily. "You were born to wear the gondolier's straw hat."

He glistened with perspiration, his profile shimmering. In silhouette, he could be an Angelo or a Silvio.

He rowed powerfully. His hands, brisk and efficient in propelling the oar and slicing the water with slow strokes, were the same ones that, since they wed, had turned her over and gently removed her nightgown all slowly. She was aroused, captivated. Lying naked they were uninhibited—between lovemaking they mimed scenes from plays; lately, to arouse him, she mimed a wild woman of the *Bacchae*.

Now, reclining, she was longing for him to look at her, so they might mime in the open air, but he seemed absorbed, not thinking of her breasts or her embrace. He was talking about war games, military mastery, the genius of logistics, the placement of infantry. Suddenly, he was talking about the great victory at Cannae and pointing in the direction of the Alps, where Hannibal had crossed with six hundred elephants single file. "Germany's victory will exceed even Cannae!" he shouted, ecstatic, not to her but to the lagoon itself, and beyond to Berlin, "Cannae, inspired our war plans, taught us how to annihilate an enemy."*

A thunderstorm, like a dark phantom, rolled over Venice and brought lightning bursts to the porphyry and marble of Saint Mark's. The gleam and gold of Venice were reflected in his eyes. Ilse turned to view the drama of the storm over the city, saying, "We should never go home. We should spend our lives here. You were talking of battles. Sorry if I was not listening before. Venice enchants me—what excuse do I need?"

"You are quite perfect—just as you are. If only the rain would stop."

"If it doesn't, we shall still have the whole luscious night together."

Georg's eyes were on the horizon, and he wasn't in the mood for talking about love. He turned away when she spoke so boldly. She was raging inside, lusting for the Redentore festival and the fireworks, the thrill of it, and then Georg's body covering hers in their opulent bed at the Danieli. Her fingers felt their way to her mouth, the old, unconscious habit. She thrilled at the flashing and raging of the storm around her, the rising water charging the crumbling walls of the palazzos.

Then suddenly, relief. There was a white haze, and the rain stopped— she could see the bell tower of Saint Mark's and the brightness of the Doge's palace. Georg docked the boat at the Danieli, where two tall and exceedingly tanned gondoliers helped tie it up. As they entered the

---

* · Cannae, 216 BC. *Ludendorff,* Karl Tschuppik and W. H. Johnston.

hotel, he was handed a telegram and asked for the train schedule for the next few days. He needed to get to Berlin: The Kaiser was on holiday in Norway— there was no urgency of war—nothing would happen until the harvest was in—Serbia had to be humiliated, that was what German and Austrian diplomats wanted. For weeks, he had heard, there had been increased intelligence gathering along the Russian-Austrian frontier.** Still that had seemed a wise precaution, also a warning to Russia. Now he had the telegram cancelling his leave: he and other officers were being recalled.

Earlier, when they began their honeymoon in Milan, running and smiling, kissing cheeks and hands, removing jewelry and replacing it, Georg promised that they would see the festival of Il Redentore, the Redeemer, marking the end of the plague in the sixteenth century. Together they anticipated the fireworks, the garlanded fishing boats, the bands, the thanksgiving bridge, and the excitement of the Venetians on this feste di tutti festi.

They changed for a special dinner, after which they would take one of the tourist boats to the island of Guidecca. Already, hundreds of decorated boats were in the lagoon, with family members enjoying their holiday meal of duck or fish. Through the streets around Saint Mark's, people gathered to eat snails from stalls by the waterside, and wine was plentiful. Most walked to Guidecca over the votive bridge, prepared just for this holiday. A thrill of anticipation went through the crowd, as it waited for a boat laden with flowers, the signal of this festival beginning. Hundreds of boats were already in the lagoon.

"Shhh! Everyone, listen," Ilse said with mock seriousness to anyone in earshot, "to the roar of the Adriatic."

A few tourists froze and then realized she was teasing and laughed.

At eleven their group of tourists got on the boat to Guidecca, carrying their wine bottles and glasses, and a fellow German asked, "Shall we travel to the cemetery at San Michele tomorrow?"

"Too morbid; there are enough dead relics here," Georg said.

An American turned to him. "*Dulce et decorum est pro patria mori,*

** · Buttar, *Collision of Empires* and Clark, Christopher, *The Sleepwalkers.*

is it not? Young soldiers lie in hidden graves, their dreams of glory extinguished."

When the Venetians burst into local songs, lauding the lions of Venice and remembering old gondoliers, Georg did his best to join in. Wine was passed from boat to boat and all glasses were filled.

Suddenly, the American was sitting beside Ilse. Breathlessly, she asked, "Are you mocking my husband?"

"Why, no. He seems a perfect cavalier, with his gold-braid trimming and blue epaulettes. I shall compose a poem about the drumroll of armies; I'll dedicate poems to him, though you will think them unworthy. I have never been to battle myself. Judging by your husband's age neither has he, but he knows the seduction of the parade ground, the sweet bonding with fellow officers. Interesting, you are visiting Venice for—"

She was already ahead of him, replying to his question. "For our honeymoon; and if you need to know more, we are from Berlin, and my husband's a lieutenant."****

Americans were so direct, so bold, rather dashing. She liked him and wondered if Georg would be jealous.

Georg was behind her in the boat; to whom was he talking? Why wasn't he beside her? Was he flirting, making an assignation? She could not free herself from this man, but she was amused—she didn't want to flee. Boatmen greeted them as they disembarked on Guidecca. Thinking she and the American were a couple, they teased them, "Kiss, kiss, tourists. You must kiss each other!" and the poet put his arms around her and kissed her. It seemed like all Venice was now on Guidecca, waiting to see the fireworks.

As the American placed his calling card in her hand, he squeezed it. "Stephen Walsh, poet, resident at the Albergo Bellissima Venezia, a humble rooming house in the Dorsudoro district. I shall be pleased to visit you," he shouted over the din. "I will also compose a poem for you if you will visit me, Signora—"

"Eddings. We are at the Danieli. How long will you be in Venice?"

*** Georg would have been a Leutnant in the Imperial German Army – a rank equivalent to second lieutenant

As they were speaking, the crowd, as one body, proceeded to the Church of Il Redentore, led by the bishop in purple regalia, holding a crozier.

A roar of excitement interrupted their conversation, as the first fireworks, gold and red, illuminated the sky. Ilse was jolted by the noise and the crowd shouting, and her hands grabbed Walsh's. He was surprised that she had removed her gloves, and he did the same.

Near midnight, the fireworks ended, and the crowd, excited but hushed, waited for the bishop and altar boys to begin the Mass at the church.

The crowd would have separated them, but Walsh held her elbow tightly, gallantly, "I will stay in Venice as long as my money holds out and I can give lectures, which I have been doing for the last month. Imagine! I give talks about the ancients, and people actually pay to hear me."

"I will believe anything of a man wearing a pink jacket and green trousers." She laughed gaily, almost with abandon.

"Ah, that is my disguise—I hide the sadness in my heart. Luckily, my patroness is a contessa who finds my poetry worth some *lire*. Everything is for sale in Venice—beware of its allure. What seems like kindness often hides a dark intent. Money-grubbers abound, and sophisticated peddlers are dressed in finery."

Ilse was intoxicated by the festival and by Walsh's attention, and was a bit drunk too. Feeling heady and emotional, she surprised herself by confessing the break with her family, the scandal of Georg's apostasy, and their marriage. Walsh was attentive; he had long wavy black hair, worn loose and he concentrated his light blue eyes on her. She imagined women liked him; she liked him.

She confessed, "I feel so guilty, for I shamed my own family in their community. I cannot go backward, but I would, if it were possible. Do you understand? If I could rip apart this new belief, I would do it—but I believe."

Suddenly, Georg emerged and took her hand. In an instant, he introduced himself and discovered that Walsh was a respectable scholar and poet. "We are going to Burano Monday, and we would be happy to have our gondolier bring you round to our hotel. It's our last day in Venice."

"Ah," said Walsh, "but love keeps me attached during the day … the Lesbia that keeps me—my wages."

"Why, Lesbia is notorious," Georg said, smiling. "It's an obligation to insult her."

Ilse had found a dear friend, and here Georg was stealing him. Two antiquarians together—they had almost forgotten her. She sat on a rock nearby as they quoted from Catullus and Horace.

People started drifting back to the bridge, either drunk or sleepy from holiday making.

We'll be out all night, she thought as the two men passed around a wine bottle.

After two hours of nonstop talk, they finally reached the end of the Roman Republic, as Walsh continued, "Augustus was the executioner and the restorer of the Republic.[****] First he needed to shed blood, more blood. He was shrewd too. Then he wrought peace, and the lust for blood was suppressed. Aeneas's words always strike me:[*****]

> *If Victory grants our force in arms this day,*
> *as I think she may—may the gods decree it so—*
> *I shall not command Italians to bow to Trojans …*
> *… May both nations, undefeated, under equal laws,*
> *march together toward an eternal pact of peace.*

Georg replied, "Yes, with peace, Augustus made Rome the beautiful marble city. Suetonius is not kind to him, but Augustus brought Rome peace, and poetry flourished. It was a golden age for 'the man who is pure of heart.' Do you collect Roman coins? I have some beautiful coins with Augustus's portrait. A few such coins pushed me to start collecting in earnest, mostly silver and bronze coins."

[****] · Tom Holland, *Dynasty*, chapter "The Godfather."

[*****] · *The Aeneid*, translated by Robert Fagles, book 12, verses 223–228.

Silver denarius of Augustus, Rome, 13 B.C.

By now, the soldiers, the local families, and the tourists were returning to their boats, and Walsh bowed and whispered, "The gods attend thee. Beware of omens—Venice is a place full of superstitions. I hope I didn't offend you, Milady. Beware of indiscretion." He came so close to her, his chin almost touching hers, that—flustered—Ilse extended her hand as she had seen Sara do, but Walsh bowed and kissed her neck instead. She was slightly drunk, she wanted to be alone with Georg, she wanted him to be kissing her.

Their boat had left the island, and so they returned by the votive bridge and approached the Danieli in a murky fog.

Walsh said to Georg, "I consider you a friend. Find merriment in Venice. Let its sensuality envelop you, young man."

The two men were engrossed, Walsh talking of Romantic poets in Venice, their mistresses, the lives cut short, while Ilse, tired, took a last step off the bridge, and her heel caught on its edge. She slipped on her elbow and was quickly up, with merely her glove torn. For an instant, she recalled Sara's tripping, how their friendship began, and then she thought no more of it. She hadn't heard from Sara and had almost forgotten her. But she was confused and intoxicated—and disturbed by the memory. There was a roaring about her. It wasn't the Adriatic; it was in her head, but she was too sleepy to think about it or about Walsh's warning of omens.

In his room, as daylight spread orange rays on Venice, Walsh wrote to a fellow poet in London:

12 July, Venezia
Hlo holy Sir Reggie,

It has been insufferably hot so that I wondered why I came to Venice in summer. Rain and thunder. Yet the fztival yesterday was a success, Redentore. I met a young Hun Jewish RC woman—I want to write this so I never forget it, Jewish Catholic, or so she intends, torn up about her beliefs, so I told her the pagans had it right and she was unnecessarily anxious. Drawn by pageantry into RC, your mummery, art, the music &c. She bewitched me with her ivory hands, which I touched, in the dark as we spoke, her hair mussed, disorderly, as her hat slid sideways. Why doesn't America have such lovely women? Here the women are marvelous, even the tourists.

Provokingly she is married, no chance to tryst in a curtained gondola, what a caress that would be. I would kiss her eyes, her lips, her ivory hands. I write this so as not to forget it. She, whom I momentarily adore, married to a Hun, a Protestant! But he is also a Jew. I still cannot believe this is in the name of religion! I should create a satire out of this religious concoction. In dactylic hexameter.

The angel with tears tells me about a family dispute, faith, the nature of Christ, oh dear God. Ghastly—dead serious, it takes all the charm out of life to be so damned glum, leeching dynamism and spontaneity out of everything. Yet suddenly she is transformed into a delicious creature, invents tales, elves, headless heroes & shadowless princesses.

She has doubts and anxieties which I would brush away. Criminal that her husband dznot. Perhaps it suits him that she depndz wholly on him. Banished, family tiff about religion &c., hard words, sadness, reconciliation, rash decision to marry at the Registry.

Husband attached to the German General Staff, and so secretive. Tried to talk about cooperation with England, but he only repeated headlines of morning paper. He changes suddenly when talk of antiquity, and we were damned lively. At the mere mention of Catullus or Polybius, the husband is absolutely warm, wants to interpret the Punic Wars, recite Latin poetry, and reinvents himself as an enthusiastic classicist. Is he a blood lusting Hun militarist, as I first supposed? Is he a passive Jew, in his soul, a heretic?

All this revealed in one evening, to me, the greatest carouser! Now is this epic, tragedy or comedy? I advised him to have a fug, a good fug, with a Venetian courtesan, lay down his heavy load, listen to the gondoliers' lusty songs. Then I might seduce his young bride, but no, they must return to Germany, for war, he fears, is imminent.

Soon La contessa will call—I must to sleep … pray to dream of Frau Ilse!

Yours,
Fuggin' Walsh

***

Ilse was extraordinarily happy, the festival had been perfect, she was struck by the serenity of the priest and his altar boys in the midst of the holiday atmosphere. When they returned to the Danieli, Ilse and Georg made love late into the night, and Georg fell asleep with his arm covering her.

"Wake up," Ilse whispered in Georg's ear, even though they had just barely gone to sleep. His arm, sticky and damp, was covering her, and their guide was waiting.

"Islands, remember? Our last day in Venice, soon to pack and return to Berlin, to the mighty Reich and its duties," she said, disentangling herself. He turned and she kissed him lightly, saying she would call for coffee.

She hesitated, wondering if she should wait for him to agree, and then decided they both needed coffee. The young waiter, who always watched her from the corners of the hotel, brought their breakfast. She teased him, called him Romeo. It was a last full day in Venice, and after she enjoyed her coffee, she took her sun hat and went down to the hotel entrance to wait for Georg, choosing a spot where the young waiter might observe her.

Signor Visentini, their guide, gossiped with the hotel manager until Georg, weaving a path, came down the stairs and lurched to the gondola.

As usual, Silvano was cursing another gondolier, something to do with their mothers—it happened every day.

Georg was awake now, and Signor Visentini offered, "Shall we go to the lace school on Burano?"

The lagoon was bright blue-green, the morning smell acceptable; the gondola moved into the dewy heat, and Silvano began a romantic song.

Hued brown and black, at first Burano was disappointing—the walkways crumbling, with garbage strewn by the water's edge. A wounded bird, its beak bloodied, found sanctuary in the cracked cement, half of its body protruding, and Ilse recoiled. Signor Visentini, with a sure motion lifted the bird, "We'll take the sandpiper to the school, they'll save it."

The lacemaking school, a brick edifice, formerly a palazzo, was encircled by huddled buildings, poor fishermen's homes. In the courtyard, students worked together, mostly with needles, some with tweezers, the day's exercise was *punto in aria*.

Signor Visentini—who was immeasurably proud of Venice, though it might be sinking and putrid, with moss growing on the palazzos—was eager to explain about the lace school and the history of Burano lace. He was rewarded for his effort when travelers showed an appreciation for Venice, the revival of old crafts and handiwork. His entire family, in-laws included, was Venetian; one of his sisters was a nun in Venice. He told his family history to foreigners who enjoyed hearing about local life. He knew the myriad residents of Venice, the nobility, the crafts workers, the expatriates, and the prostitutes.

Until the eighteenth century, he explained, the girls who traditionally specialized in lace were impoverished orphans, but these young girls were receiving a stipend, and the designer, a young woman, a graduate of an arts school, had a proper salary. Ilse wondered what she had thought about when she was the age of the girls, cavorting in the Frisian Sea, not responsible for anyone, buried in warm sand in Norderney as Georg and Walther played nearby with Leon and let him win at marbles. Leon loved their attention, and his sheer joy at being accepted was catching; it made the family whole. Her poor brother had been so uncoordinated, stooped over, and Georg had made him happy. Why was she thinking of that?

At the end of a row of lacemakers, the designer was drawing at an easel, absorbed and focused. Ilse approached, asking in heavily accented Italian if she might take a closer look. On the sketch pad, the girl was drawing birds in frenzied motion, while on the side were butterflies ensnared in webs, trying to break free.

"Do you have a pattern book?" Ilse asked.

The girl pointed to her forehead.

"You're such an artisan and yet so young!" Ilse exclaimed. "Is your mother a lacemaker?"

"I'm an orphan, signora."

Signor Visentini walked over, churning the crumbling cement with his heavy step. "These designs are for unique tinted laces. Signorina Adriana creates the designs for the school, and the *maestra* presents the completed laces to Queen Margherita, who gifts them to patronesses who want something unusual for the social season. After a year or two, the designs are available to others."

Ilse envied such an imagination that could hide the form of animals and wild vegetation in arabesques, the intricate tracery of it. Adriana was daring—taking risks in her designs.

"Tell me about this design," Ilse pressed.

"It's a fantasy. I'll design a special mantilla with the image of the Virgin Mary, for you."

Adriana tore off the sheet she was cartooning, placing it on her stool, and sketched. She looked intently at Ilse, rose abruptly, and returned with color wash, a brush, and graphite. She drew a pattern that initially appeared merely craftsman-like, but then, hidden in an arabesque, Ilse saw the Virgin's profile, the wash its golden halo, then the image was concealed by fine graphite lines.

When Georg walked over, the Virgin's profile was already hidden, but he sensed an unusual special beauty, without being able to see it. "With that mantilla framing your face," he said, "you'll surely be noticed."

"Oh, no," Ilse said, "I should be the most humble of God's creatures. It's an omen. Venice is full of omens and magic, as Walsh said. I am unworthy of that design."

"The girl wants you to have something beautiful, something unique, and so do I," Georg said. "Don't deny me that pleasure. I will ask the maestra, Signora Marcetti, to have a mantilla made of this design."

Ilse walked away and stood with Signor Visentini. Georg lingered by Adriana, whose full lips, he noticed, were red and shiny, as if smeared in jelly. He waited there foolishly, unsure what to do. Was he to find gifts for their parents, for Ilse's sister?

He was embarrassed in front of these young girls.

Signor Visentini came up to him. "Herr Eddings, let's make an end of this. The girls need to continue their work. You should order the mantilla from the maestra, and when it reaches Berlin, your wife will be delighted."

Staving off doubt, Georg approached the maestra. "That sketch for my wife, can your lacemakers weave it?"

Just then, one of the young girls walked over to Ilse. Ringlets of black hair escaped the girl's bonnet. She put her arm around Ilse. "We have been waiting for you to make this mantilla. It will be so fine. For prayer—it will be perfect. Do not be afraid."

The girl continued, "I know your heart," and walked away.

Walsh had said Venice was full of magic, omens, and superstitions. Now Ilse understood.

The maestra wrapped some gifts, napkins with lace borders, a runner for a tea caddy, lace trimmed handkerchiefs. She promised to send the mantilla—that special girl would weave it—and it would be done in a month, she said.

Returning to the gondola, Ilse gripped Georg's hand tightly. "I must visit a convent here." The lace makers had stirred up her religious fervor, which had diminished after the civil ceremony, so banal, and been totally suppressed as she navigated her new life. She was ready to make the leap of faith, on the verge, trembling, and stood up in the gondola, as Burano receded.

"Signora," Signor Visentini said, "you'll fall into the lagoon like that."

"Ilse, you're competing with the gondolier," said Georg. "Come sit by me."

Warmed by the Mediterranean sun, his eyes unaccustomed to its strong rays, Georg scrutinized the face he loved. He saw her dilated nostrils, the compressed lips, the fingers at her mouth. What was amiss? She had embarrassed him—she must have known it—and she seemed indifferent.

That love could be suspended, that it could expand and contract, and that this moment might indeed be critical surprised Georg. Perhaps as he rose in rank as an officer, Ilse might embarrass him, rather than enhance his reputation. Would such a thing happen, as it had now on Burano? Would there be times when he would doubt his newly wedded wife?

***

Back at the hotel, Georg watched as Ilse removed her hat, her ribbons, her muslin dress, and at last her corset. She was like a precious pearl, and he vowed that he would love her passionately forever. She was already half asleep, while he felt alive and eager and warm. Within minutes, she was sleeping peacefully. He lay down beside her, blowing gently on the strands of hair that fell across her face. He tried to move her slightly toward him, but she was sound asleep. Excitement was building in his body, hard and impossible to ignore, yet he was unable to rouse Ilse. His wife was enticing but oblivious, and Walsh's suggestion of Venetian courtesans rang in his ears.

Georg left the hotel, walking quayside, and then began walking north toward S. Maria de Formosa, passing local Venetians. He was sorry the honeymoon was ending, yet his destiny was to protect his homeland. He had entered the academy at just the right time and would already be a commander if war erupted. He was very young and very strong, and he was thrilled—he would be a hero. He was walking quickly, yet paused to look at the people in the square, at some young boys jostling each other.

An elegant young woman was coming toward him, in a tight bodice, with lace sleeves, a flounced skirt trimmed in lace, and high-buttoned leather boots. She wore a lace-straw cutaway hat, which shaded her eyes, and he saw her smile widely, and at the same moment took in her very red lips, and he knew it was Adriana.

"What a lucky chance that we should meet here," she said.

He realized right away that he would make love to her and that it would be ecstatic; he could tell she knew it too. He guessed from her expression that she wasn't surprised to see him; her clothes, her shiny lips, her movement toward him, all expressed desire. They both had to make polite conversation first.

"May I walk with you, Signorina Adriana? My wife fell asleep. The festival and the morning trip tired her out."

"One needs to be used to the heat. I thought your wife was afraid. Gentle people can get exhausted when they sense how fragile Venice is. They sleep or weep."

He wondered where she had learned these lines; she recited them by rote, he thought. He asked, "Do you live around here?"

"Oh my, no." She laughed at that, flicking him with her free hand. The other hand held a very large purse. "Working people live in Mestre. I come here for the school's patronesses or rich tourists; they choose patterns they like and then donate to the school. Today, the maestra sent me here to show patterns to an important English lady," and she pointed to her bag.

"You're very talented," he said. He felt he could not wait; he was in a rush to be with her alone, even in a hidden alley. Thinking of what Walsh said about courtesans, he was embarrassed. Her face glowed, as she intuited and welcomed his desire.

"Let me carry your bag and accompany you, Signorina."

"Adriana," she whispered in his ear, as if she were revealing an intimate secret. He felt her tongue in his ear. Was she making fun of him?

She hastened to make him easy, "I have to return to Burano later, but I know an inn where they have special Venetian appetizers. I love to eat those fish, and I'm famished. Shall we go there?"

Now far from the bright colors circling Saint Mark's, Georg felt a certain relief, mixed with panic. He suddenly preferred not to be in control, to be led away, down the cobblestoned streets, over another bridge to another quarter where few tourists came.

At the inn, he realized how hungry he was, and they both greedily ate the sardines and octopus the wizened owner placed before them, as three cats paced around them. Climbing the stairs to the third floor, Adriana told him about her family—just enough for Georg to understand she was poor, and that too sounded like a rehearsed lesson.

In the sparse room, with a bed, a chamber pot, and a chair, she undressed quickly and then, completely nude, said, "Let's lie down together for a little while." She explored him, folded herself around him, and then asked, "Can you play the flute for me?" She had no shame, and he didn't have to be gentle. He experimented, tried a position he had heard about from fellow officers, and wished the moments would last and last.

Adriana declared, "I didn't go to the patron; I followed you. First, I had to wait twenty minutes for you to come out of the hotel. I was sure your wife would go to sleep; it happens all the time. I walked behind you, with a veil, watching your buttocks sway. Nice. Think what this is worth."

He had to laugh, and as she nipped and licked him, he forgot the drumroll of armies, the Prussian military machine. By midafternoon, she had to return to work; she still had to go to the patron. They cleaned themselves with the sheet, and she took his money clip and counted.

He watched her concentration as she extracted all his lire, except a few with which he would pay the old innkeeper. They parted near the front door, where he handed the rest of the money to the old man. Then, formally, Adriana said, "A perfect afternoon, Signor Eddings. I will make sure the mantilla is exquisite," and she turned away and headed west.

****

When she did not find Georg, Ilse cornered their guide, sweetly, with a last request, a final whim. "You said your sister is in a convent, and I would like to meet her."

"Gladly, signora. It will be a long walk." She was undeterred.

"Silvano and I are at your disposal, and we'll take the gondola," the guide said, bemused and with exaggerated politeness.

At the Camaldolese convent, she ascended the steps, slimy with green brown algae, and heard the screeching of a pulley which opened the door to the *piano nobile,* the first floor. A dwarf like nun met Ilse and put her gnarled hands over Ilse's young, unblemished hands. "Please enjoy the garden and wait," she said, leading Ilse to a bench in an attached garden. "Sister Maria Cristina is just finishing up in the kitchen."

An old white sheepdog loped towards Ilse, rolling over in front of her. Ilse was in a brilliant expectant mood, and, as the dog was playful and good company, she rubbed her belly. The sun was bright and the day at its hottest when Ilse finally sat down with Sister Maria Cristina, who had a genteel air, an oval face like Ilse's, and remarkably smooth skin. It struck Ilse that the nun smiled no matter what was said. Despite the bulky habit, she appeared very thin, and since only her face and hands were visible, Ilse immediately noticed her long fingers.

"Aha, you've met Miranda, our sheepdog," said Sister Maria Cristina, as the dog ambled away to lie in the shade. Smiling, she took Ilse into the library, where the dwarf like nun brought two glasses of water. "Would you like to see the photos and books we have of our Holy Father's visit here?" The scrapbooks were filled with photos of the nuns and postulants, and of Pope Pius X's visit to the conventual church.

Ilse was distracted as Sister Maria Cristina spoke or hummed or sang. "I love to sing and joined this order because of the singing at their masses.

"We have had many guests here—you would be surprised. Tourists like you come to Venice and then want to flee the crowds. Look, here is a letter from our Holy Father, thanking us for our graciousness. Such goodness is in him, to thank us, when we should thank him for visiting us."

Ilse could hardly get in a word, let alone explain what had drawn her here and what she needed most of all. *Please stop with the photos, please stop with the letter,* she wanted to shout, but she could hardly say she was not interested.

"When our Holy Father was here," crowed Sister Maria Cristina, "so many dignitaries came to the island, and the children in the school sang for him, and he acknowledged each student by name!"

Ilse wanted to visit the chapel, but Sister Maria Cristina moved toward a meeting room. "Come hear our children practicing for Sunday."

A hefty sister, playing piano, was arranging the girls, all in blue uniforms, for harmonies, and the young girls were saying *yes, sister* and *thank you, sister* again and again. Ilse sat with Sister Maria Cristina as the girls sang three hymns to Mary, lifting their faces, following the nun's directions, looking up with piety, their eyes glistening. Ilse held back tears, because just a few years before she had been as eager as they were. She had expected, certainly prayed for, a renewed religious ecstasy from the visit to the convent. As the rehearsal concluded Ilse's heart contracted, for she would not be able to speak about her belief in Christ and in the sacraments. Sister Maria Cristina did not give her an opening and she was too self-conscious.

The sun was setting and the sky streaked with grey clouds, "Oh, but it's so late," Sister Maria Cristina smiled. "My dear, it has been wonderful to meet you. I must tell you we have a spare room for guests; if you come to Venice again, perhaps you might stay with us. I know my brother will want to get you back to your hotel before dinnertime, but it has been so good of you to visit us. Keep Christ in your heart, and avoid temptation in thought or deed. There are many temptations for a young woman, pretty as you are, going about so independently. St Paul tells us: 'Set your affection on things above, not on things on the earth.'"(Colossians 3:2 KJV)

In Germany, it had seemed so easy. She had felt God's presence, she was drawn to Jesus, and she had known what she was doing was right. She knew that was why she encountered those pilgrims near Bad Kötzting. She longed to be inspired. She had imagined kneeling with the nun, having a strong spiritual experience in Venice, reciting prayers together with the nuns. She had yet to make the leap to convert; she had hoped for much from this visit to the convent, to feel part of the community. *The nuns would strengthen her resolve*, she thought; *they would placate her guilt toward her family*. Yet they weren't especially attentive to her, they weren't impressed by her faith, they had to complete their daily routine, teach children, and made no fuss over her.

Already Signor Visentini was waiting for her at the gondola. Silvano was singing an inoffensive ballad. She had hoped for an epiphany, to feel like she did when the pilgrims had called to her.

When Sister Maria Cristina waved goodbye, the tiny nun, the gatekeeper, turning the wheel for the pulley, said "We will pray my dear that you find your faith. Read St. Francis' Canticle when you can, it will help you. Do not be discouraged for 'now we only see through a glass darkly but then face to face.'" (I Corinthians 13:12 KJV)

There was nothing to do but go down the slimy steps, on which Signor Visentini was shining a light.

It was dusk, a dark end to the day and the honeymoon.

On the train the following morning, returning to Berlin, she wept in disappointment. She was not sure what she expected from her visit to the convent. If it was her purpose to become more devout, she had failed. In just two years, Ilse had brought grief to her parents—who forgave her, thinking it their mission to save her. Perhaps Annette and Martin, who were so pleased with their baby, were right. Ingrate, *apikoros*, they called her. Then too she was troubled for she sensed a change in Georg. He was different, thinking of the farewells in Berlin, the promises of a battlefield, glory, bravery, honor. She thought how lonely she would be, while he would belong to other people now.

In the train, Georg hugged his wife, wiped away two tears from her heavy-lidded eyes and shuddered slightly.

"Why did you shiver?" she asked.

"You know the saying—you shiver when someone walks over your grave," he laughed.

14

October 1914

Squinting, Georg had marched east through Prussian towns and farms and through Polish swamps. The Eighth Army marched for days, fifty kilometers a day, in the scorching August sun, bathing in the Masurian lakes. The sockets of soldiers' eyes hurt; their eyelids itched endlessly. Georg's sunburned nose and neck matched his hair, he heard every possible joke about redheads. In September they were drenched and the armies fought in a sea of mud. The Germans pushed the Russians back, then the Russian army defeated the Germans forcing them to retreat. Then they did it all over again as the front moved back and forth several times.

Singed by flames, his dusty uniform torn, he ached when a comrade was killed, when an armless soldier screamed, or when, lying in muck, a wounded soldier bled, waiting for medics to come. Flare lights shone in the inky darkness, men yelled, "Get the wounded out!," "Medics, over here!," "Kill the bastards!," "Forward!"

German artillery on the battlefield

Sometimes there was silence, and he scribbled stories for <u>Undertone</u>, "We need to keep up morale," Georg told his men, "even if you never wrote before, try to report on something you saw." Every man in the unit was helping with the paper, writing or sketching or helping in the field press. Georg contributed, put his thoughts into meter, sometimes printing only fragments, especially during the fighting at Gumbinnen and Allenstein.

Abruptly reassigned to teach at the military academy in Berlin—by Ludendorff, no less—he took the notepad on which he had begun his stories, hoping to finish them now, with Ilse's help. In his satchel were her letters, some fretful, others humorous, with cartoons of events at home, short rants about the demand for sugar, drawings of his coins, details of her new work at the museum—which completely absorbed her. He thought, *she's lyrical, inspired*. Her life was full of magical dreams and hopes. In his pocket were lines he had written:

Hot breezes blew caps away.
The best of us lie in unmarked graves,
Bootless, headless men, now rising with the dew.
We want to live—let us live, procreate, and die peacefully.
Let us have wives, children—let us tell our grandchildren tales.
A soldier lusted for death;
He rushed out from hiding—gray silhouetted against the sun.
Enemy fire murdered his battalion.
A bearded fellow who snatched the Iron Cross.

Perhaps, if Ilse read such lines, she would understand him, understand about the war, ripped bodies, mines exploding, flames, barbed wire.

His lips curled sardonically as he imagined the figure he must have cut at Gumbinnen, his arm flourishing an old-fashioned lance, striking blows, splendidly stabbing, sensing his strength, his virility. He brought all his power to bear to topple Poles and Cossacks from their Don horses; horses fled swiftly as the enemy disappeared in fog and smoke. He shoved aside wounded soldiers, pursued the backs of the enemy. He remembered a horse split in two, and then his troops, trapped in a salient, suddenly turning and pushing past him, driven back to the Vistula. He struggled a Russian soldier to the ground, shot him, seized a riderless horse, and galloping fiercely, escaped.

A dead Russian soldier

The train home streaked past farms and towns, passing woods, lakes and wooden houses. He ached to rush home to Ilse. Finally he was in Berlin, at Schlesischer Station. The station was crowded with departing soldiers; it was impossible not to bump into them. There were tearful couples, mothers hugging their sons. A solitary mother, waving a gloved hand at a train bound east, reminded Georg of his own mother. He shuddered, remembering her warm fur coats. As a child, he had hidden under those coats, her warm body protecting him from wind and cold.

There was no singing now at the station, no cornucopia of chocolates or cigarettes. Mere weeks before, young girls had thrown flowers at the departing soldiers, and rifles had been adorned with lilies as thousands of Germans celebrated with thousands of beers, singing patriotic songs.

Georg's badge glinted; his epauletted shoulders distinguished him and soldiers respectfully saluted him. He saluted back smartly. He had a rush of good feeling, a sense of pride.

Two German soldiers

He stopped in a café for weisswurst and onions, chased with beer. The smell of caraway from the seeded rolls evoked his childhood, and he heard a soldier tell a well-worn joke: "How long will the war last? Till the officers have the same food as the men." *A rite of passage*, he thought.

He looked out the café window at somber faces, hard-working civilians going about their business. He admired the women; they seemed so purposeful. Walking by was an old man, checking his pocket watch—bending to pet his bulldog, a brindle beast with short legs. Georg loved these people; they were his people; he was protecting them, their way of life. He wanted to embrace everyone he saw. He had just barely mastered being a commander, sure of his decisions, disdaining outmoded ways of fighting. The swiftness with which the battle had developed at Gumbinnen, the speed with which the Russians were outflanked at Allenstein still amazed him.

As passersby admired him he thought, *if they had seen me command the gunners they would have been astonished*. He moved amiably after his beer and sausage, strolling into a beer garden. It was midafternoon, and the tables were just filling up. He should be going home to see Ilse; she would be happy to see him. He bought another beer. It was so very good.

"Did you see how that pretty woman came up to me?" a young man was saying to a friend. "She was just throwing herself at me!"

"They've all become so interesting with their husbands gone. A woman flung herself at me last night and took me to her villa in Friedrichstrasse. You should have seen the place, all inlaid furniture and chandeliers. That woman was so hungry!"

This second young man abruptly turned to Georg and held out his hand. "Herr Leutnant, just back from the front? We're honored to meet you. We work in the factory that manufactures the opticals for rifles. They could not spare us, but we both want to sign up. What's it like?"

Georg wanted to fill his story with glory, with exhilarating victories. He could tell them about fierce fighting, ambushes and heroic soldiers; that was what they wanted to hear. Yet different words spilled out, sentences he hadn't uttered at the front. "We lost a lot of men in the first weeks; the Russian First Army ranged against us and we were outnumbered three to one. The officers thought the war on the Eastern Front was already lost. So many young soldiers and old reservists were killed. Our own East Prussian towns were deserted, houses and barns burned. As we passed tormented German farmers and their frightened families, carrying their belongings on wagons, scrambling to reach West Prussia, soldiers wept. In those first early battles we were driven back."

He had suppressed the memory of the ghost towns, the burned villages; the tales of atrocities, of Germans garroted, women raped, Cossack plunder. Half the tales were not true, exaggerated, he knew, but they got combined with the pursuit by the Russian army, the machine gun barrages, and his artillery company covering a German retreat. He had made uplifting and inspiring speeches to his unit when leaving Königsberg. ("We are a proud German army, strong and invincible. Our sacrifices have been for our country. There is no nobler cause.") He wanted to win these men over by saying, "We beat the shit out of them" or "We busted their balls". He started to explain the logistics, the military plan, the heavy artillery bombardment. Finally, to stop himself, he concluded stiffly, "In the end, we returned an eye for an eye. They fought hard, the Russian soldiers, they were good men, totally lacking modern batteries. Our guns and mortars were just so much better."

"Oh, *Quatsch*," one of the young men said. " We saw a newsreel –they're dirty Slavs. Their army beaten thanks to Hindenburg, our hero – everyone hears about Tannenberg. Yet why take prisoners of war? 100,000 scum! Should have been shot dead." One giggled, the other smirked. They despised Slavs. They only knew about German superiority and valor. "Officer, make a toast with us," they raised their mugs, "To the great Hindenburg."

He no longer wanted his beer. He could not hear himself over the din anyway. He left the café and strode toward Unter den Linden. He had accepted the gloom by the station, but in the Tiergarten district, the streets were bright and cheerful and cafés were full. Well-dressed couples passed him, and women walked hand in hand, smartly turned out in autumn dresses, shoes sparkling. Bankers in vested suits and bowler hats and dandies in fedoras passed him. There were even carriages—hadn't the army requisitioned the horses? There was a party atmosphere and unconsciously he clenched his fists.

Perhaps he might visit his parents first, to overcome his anger; they were always supportive, and their apartment was closer.

His father, how old he seemed, embraced him warmly. "My young Leutnant!"

"We did not let the Russians crush us, Papa. Despite the enemy's superior forces, the victory was ours. It was a hard won victory. As we passed the ruins of Teutonic castles, I saw them as a powerful symbol, and suggested to General Ludendorff to christen it the Battle of Tannenberg, redeeming our honor where Teutonic knights were humiliated in 1410. Certainly resonates better, than say, the battle of Allenstein or Frögenau."[*]

"Splendid idea! It's already catching on —Berliners say the Battle of Tannenberg will force our enemies to beg for peace."

---

[*] It was probably General von Hindenburg who suggested the name Tannenberg to the Kaiser. Hindenburg was known as the hero of Tannenberg.

Georg bowed to his father, "I hope so, sir." Then he asked, "Bought any new coins?" This tied parents and son together—their fascination with ancient coins and medals. Georg had been homesick for these conversations, and though tired, was happy to talk about numismatics again.

"Yes, some, but nothing spectacular," his father said. "There are marvelous medals that we are studying for a client. The Morgenson collection is being catalogued, and your mother and I have plaster casts of their Renaissance medals. Would you like to see them?"

While his mother plied him with sandwiches and coffee, his father laid out the casts and photographs, saying, "Germany is the beacon of the enlightened world, just as these humanists were in their time. Look at these marvelous medals of Medicis!"

Georg was tempted to stay there all night, but that would not do; they would suppose he did not want to go home.

"This piece looks like a Leone Leoni," he said. *Such a violent man, Leoni*, George thought. *A murderer, perhaps, yet a consummate artisan.*

"Yes, it does. Most likely it's from his workshop."

For a long time, they sat and talked about the flowering of art in the fifteenth century; about early Renaissance culture; about the provenance of medals, Pisanello's artistry, his designs of lions and unicorns.

His parents told him that after they introduced Ilse to a director at the Altes Museum, she successfully took over several responsibilities. Georg lingered, and then they had a late dinner, his mother serving a favorite sweet dish. "Listen, Georg," she said kindly, yet concerned too, "unless you are going to sleep here, you should go home. Does Ilse even know you are in Berlin?"

A few minutes later, Georg gave his father an affectionate handshake. His father saluted him, singing out as Georg left, "Victory, victory."

Georg moved closer to his apartment on Dreysestrasse. The Berlin night wind, tamer than the howling winds at the front, blew behind his back. He had been comfortable looking at the medals, but now he was fatigued. He recognized the windows of their apartment, the curtains drawn; the dark building illuminated by a gas streetlight. Ilse would be surprised, and she would want to dance. Yes, that is how he remembered her—dancing, whirling, flirting.

He unlatched the apartment door and then put his knapsack down silently. Ilse was fast asleep; her head turned sideways, her mouth slightly open.

He removed his boots and cap, but was so tired that, still dressed, he lay down beside her, watching her and inhaling her scent. Slowly, she turned toward him, and they kissed. Everything was happening slowly, slowly, the way he liked it. He was terribly tired, he suddenly realized. His legs were tired, his arms almost numb as he undressed.

They held each other, savoring their love, slowly, and ecstatically. She wanted to spar in bed, to mug for him and laugh together, but he was exhausted.

"We'll dance tomorrow."

She kissed him tenderly and laughed. "You are a handsome prince from a faraway continent, so dark, with brown raccoon eyes!"

His worries and anxieties dissipated. He fell asleep in her arms, and now he slept deeply and dreamlessly, as he had not done for eight weeks.

When Ilse woke him, very eager, he imagined himself in her eyes and let her lead him in dancing. They made love again and fell back asleep together.

Over coffee, he tried to tell her about the first battles. "There was a barrage, a bullet grazed me, Russians broke through, I was sure they had me, but suddenly my sergeant, Arthur, scrambled, cried out, 'Leutnant, I'll get you behind the lines.' It was dark but I realized these Russians had no weapons, before I could yell out, Arthur killed them. I was saved, but I shuddered in horror. Dear God! They were just boys. I was delirious, but I was praying. I prayed that we would have a child. I survived this time, but next time? The fear is terrible yet it is all worth it to have a child."

At this, Ilse looked at him with an expression he could not read.

15

Late October 1914

Georg had been home for a few days, teaching at the academy. Friday morning, Ilse said, "It will be nice Sunday. After Mass, Heidi and I will have lunch in Grunewald. The autumn leaves out there should be beautiful. Will you come?"

"Who is Heidi?" Georg asked.

"My colleague, Heidi."

"Colleague?" Georg replied with a snort. He thought, *she's being ridiculous using a term like colleague— why she just began working at the museum and she can't seriously be thinking of a career. As soon as the men come back, they'll have their posts back.*

On Sunday, Heidi was waiting at Saint Michael's Church. She was plain, bespectacled, tall, and broad. As they approached the church, Ilse said, "She's an illustrator. She has the delicate touch of a miniaturist and the patience of one too. She also photographs the museum collection, especially for the catalogue. And she's a devoted Lutheran; she helps everyone; she never refuses to do a favor. So that we might meet, she went to her church's early service this morning."

Heidi extended her hand, as a man would, before he even reached her. "Welcome, Lieutenant Eddings. Ilse has told me so much about you. I'm so glad to meet you."

Georg immediately liked her.

"Perhaps you would help me? I was hired to prepare a series of illustrations for posters encouraging civilians to buy war bonds. The graphics should look authentic, create a story. You've had first-hand experience – I want to draw images of danger and heroism. Ilse says you have a gift for description, for the telling detail."

Leaving them behind, Ilse entered the slowly filling church, her Venetian veil covering her head. The Introit began, and a small choir, its numbers clearly depleted by the war, began a hymn in four-part harmony. Then the door to the vestibule closed. Georg would have liked to peer through the leaded glass and see where Ilse was. Would she approach the altar? He thought, *surely she wouldn't take communion.*

"I'd be happy to help," he replied.

"My husband and son are both on the Western front, but neither has been in combat. In their letters, they assure me all is well, and are vague about locations. I think my husband is somewhere in Flanders, in a reserve division. They sent him a few weeks ago, with the conscription of older men. I got a letter yesterday, and he wrote it's quiet where he is so bored soldiers drink and dance with local girls in taverns. My husband is a deacon at home. He reads the Bible every day, he writes. What matters is that he return home safe— do you think they will put older men in fighting units?"

Georg couldn't hear the Mass liturgy but suddenly he heard an organ piece he knew and he shuddered. Far from evoking a sense of redemption, the music evoked screams, the sight of purple-red fingers clutching a rifle, skin cut to shreds.

"What pain in your expression!" Heidi said. He was moved and embarrassed by her compassion. After a pause, she added, "What are you teaching at the academy?"

"The maneuvers of firepower, offensive and defensive. General Staff officers say Germany's artillery power will bring us victory. Perhaps your husband will be assigned an administrative task, like censoring letters. That's what most men over thirty do on the Eastern Front."

Heidi noticed how quickly he had composed himself, distancing himself from emotion. She said, "I can't absorb yet how many thousands of men have left for the front. In Berlin we're in semi-shock that the war isn't won yet. Our young men are murdered or maimed, and they murder other men. We have victories, but the war goes on. Many who never prayed are coming to church daily."

"Where they preach universal love," Georg said. "It is all around us, yet we're at war. How strange that our great ideas, our faith, our superior culture, led to this."

Someone opened the vestibule door. The Mass was ending; Georg heard chanting and shivered again. In the brightness emanating from the church he imagined light flares, saw limbs, a fist dismembered. It was Arthur, his body in muck, bleeding to death. Heidi barely heard him sigh but felt his anguish.

Heidi said, "Don't lose your faith. We must not question God—my son, reading Nietzsche endlessly, only writes that he is well fed and asks me to send him more pillows, chocolates, and cigarettes. He's confused, his ideas disturbed. My husband and I pray every day that he will turn back to the Lord." Georg saw tears welling in her eyes.

Along with the parishioners, Ilse exited the church and rushed up to them. "I knew you two would like each other. It's sunny now so let's get to Wissensee and rejoice being together."

It was indeed a nice day, and so it took a while to get one of the taxi-cabs to Grunewald. On the way, Ilse talked of work. "The illustrations for the catalogue are superb," she said to Heidi. "By next week I'll be done with the next set of abstracts. We'll probably only use one drawing for that. We should talk about our next project. I was wondering if you would like to help me with some research."

Heidi replied, "Truly, if you need an assistant, I'll gladly do it."

"All settled then," Ilse said with a smile. "I'll ask the director for permission."

Georg was amazed and confounded at this collegial behavior and bonding between women. Ilse, short, blonde, and slender, and the tall, somewhat ungainly Heidi might not have met before the war, they certainly would have been in different social circles. So different, yet they now bonded. Everything about Heidi was pleasing: her unabashed affection and concern for her husband and son, her surprising and endearing honesty.

At first, Georg was quite lively, enjoying the sun and the lake, walking under the trees.

"It's very nice of you to invite me to join you," Heidi said. As they walked by the lake it was clear that women were admiring Georg, his manly soldierly bearing, his handsomeness in his military uniform.

"Not far from here," Ilse said, "Georg proposed to me. Shall I tell you how, he jumped in the lake and then so did I. I often think of that time with great happiness," she continued as they dawdled on the path to the restaurant.

"Yes," Georg said, "We were other people then. Often in the East, I bathe in lakes quite naked, only inhibited by the fear of an enemy sniper."

As they sat down at a table, Ilse said, "I am so happy that the two people I love most are beside me. My work gives me the most pleasure, working with art. Yet at the same time I am removed from the war work. Both of you write and draw about the war, you're both making history, complementing each other, creating a culture."

"I don't do anything but repeat stories yet I agree a war culture is developing, equating manliness with fighting. I wish it weren't so, for war isn't glorious. I told you about Arthur saving me, but I didn't tell you how he felt afterwards, crying "I'm sorry" and getting ill. All his life he had been taught gentleness and mercy, and this was the first time he saw the enemy up close. The enemy as two beardless boys, maybe fifteen years old, sent to fight without weapons." Georg himself was getting emotional, so he jumped up and said he was going for a walk. He said he would compose himself and return soon, would they order schnitzel for him?

"Would you like us to join you?" Heidi asked.

"I would like to walk alone—I may find a charming, passionate *Fräulein*," he said, trying for some humor.

There it was again, Heidi thought—*his urbane manner hiding pain.*

Jokingly, she remarked "You're quite the ladies' man." As he turned away, he waved to the two women.

Ilse began shaking, "He doesn't like to talk about the war, but he's preoccupied with writing the articles. Sometimes until three in the morning. He's afraid he might be sent to France soon, and he's determined to have a child. I don't want to hold a baby on my hip, not yet."

Heidi put her arm around Ilse and said, "He's safe in Berlin; you should be glad. A child is a blessing."

"You're right. It's just been difficult," Ilse said. "It irritates him that I'm earning money. He's an excellent army officer. He belongs with his fellow soldiers. I have a chance now to be someone, part of the museum staff; it's like a dream for me. The war is turning me into someone else, don't you see, not the girl he loved. Heidi, he wants a child so much, and I'm not ready yet. I don't know what to pray for."

When they parted that evening, Heidi turned to Georg and stooping slightly, kissed him on both cheeks with warmth. When she cheek-kissed Ilse, she said, "You're blessed. How happy I would be if my Matthias were home."

16

January 1915

December was cold and grey. Berliners had been heating their homes since November but by December there was a coal shortage. January began with a freezing rain. Then thick snow hampered the movement of the taxi-cabs, and bicycling was impossible. The morning papers listed war casualties, and people scoured the pages for the names of their relatives. Ilse looked out the window at the snow-covered tree limbs, and shivered. In her trembling hand was a telegram from Leon. Walther was missing, somewhere on the Western Front.

After Ilse left Berlin, she had not seen Walther. He tried to reconcile her and Annette but Martin threatened to withdraw from the business partnership. Walther wrote, it was better not to have a family crisis, as the business supported their parents too. He would not come to her wedding. There was every chance he would soon wear Martin down. The family would meet again by January, he was sure of it. A few months later he was sent to the Western Front.

At Christmas Walther wrote asking her forgiveness, he had worried too much about Martin. His unit, he wrote, had been in a fierce and savage fight and he wanted to ask her forgiveness in case ......

Now here was Leon's sad news. Leon added she was not to worry about their parents.

Georg hugged Ilse, wrapped up in her grief and chattering with cold. "We will keep each other warm tonight." At night, she was calm, and they fell asleep with their legs entwined. At midnight, he felt the stickiness of blood, imagining for an instant he was bleeding in a dugout on the front. He felt blood on his thigh, but there was more on Ilse. She got up and turned away from him, and it was better to be quiet. He was glad that it was dark and he could not see her eyes, nor she his. The snow whirled outside as she grabbed the sheets and got up to clean herself.

Ilse would not talk about it, but when they had coffee, he held her hand. "We will try again."

"Yes," Ilse said without conviction.

Leon wrote often, he kept in touch. Annette's two boys, Jakob and Elhanan, were all smiles. Martin had turned out a good husband and a shrewd businessman, and now Moshe was so proud of this son-in-law and his grandsons that he talked of little else. Nothing more was known of Walther, Leon wrote, but Moshe and Hedwig were confident he would soon come home with a slight wound or bruise.

Ilse read the letter to Georg, "Do you suppose Walther might be missing, wounded?"

Georg said, "It's different on the Western Front, the fighting is intense in some places, it may take a while to get information. This is a savage war." Privately, he thought Walther had been blown to bits, but he didn't say any of that to Ilse. He had also heard about men wounded so badly that they did not want their families informed, and were institutionalized, bodies mangled, faces mashed up.

Later he added, "I will be sent back to the front soon. I might die. I am an only son, and without a child, my family dies out."

Ilse said, "I understand you and your parents." When she visited his parents, their eyes communicated longing and sadness.

Some days later, Ilse received a very different telegram, one that lifted her spirits. Sara Liebermann, whom Ilse had not seen since leaving Munich, was coming to Berlin.

"Would you mind staying in barracks for a few days?" Ilse asked Georg, telling him about the summer in Starnberg.

"Did you invite her to stay here?"

"I suggested she stay here—with both of us – that made her anxious. I hope you do not mind, her friendship was so important to me."

Controlling his anger, Georg thought that an officer in the Kaiser's army should remain in barracks rather than impose on his wife. He looked around at the charming apartment and then at the woman he loved. He had such pleasure caressing her. He looked longingly at her. He had wanted to apologize and explain that he would be more patient, that she needed to understand his eagerness for a child.

He did not say any of those things. "Not at all. I will stay in the barracks," he said flatly. "Has Sara Liebermann a reason to come now?"

"Why, yes, she is training with the Red Cross Frauenverein."

War changed everything. He had expected his wife to wait for him, to keep everything in order for him. He had not mocked her for her new religious fanaticism, believing it would keep her home. He had not imagined her having a vocation. Assuming Sara Liebermann's visit would be short, he looked forward to meeting her. From what Ilse had told him, she did not sound like a woman who bandaged gangrene wounds.

Has the war driven women mad? Georg asked himself. Restraining his fury, he left for the officers' casino, where he dined and got drunk.

***

"Maybe I should stay somewhere else," Sara said when Ilse met her at the station.

"Nonsense. Now, we have to hurry. It's hard to get vegetables, so we need to reach the market while there's still some choice."

Few farmers were still in the market, but Ilse found carrots, corn, many turnips, and enough potatoes for a broth.

"Do you think it will be dangerous for you among soldiers?" asked Ilse as they hurried in the cold. "You are alluring, you know that. Soldiers will reach for you."

"Stop," Sara said, her eyelashes wet. "I had to get away from Munich. Going to the front is selfish. Otherwise I would worry for myself and not get in harm's way. You know, you and your sister are to blame for what has happened." She let out a little laugh.

"Sara, that is ridiculous, but I love you, so I won't be angry. What are you talking about?" Ilse asked as they reached Dreysestrasse.

"It was because of you that I first met Claude—that time in the English Garden. The night of Dorothea's party, we danced, and afterward we met, many times. I started going to his mother's to mend my gowns, and then I pretended I needed new gowns altogether. It was easy to see him. We had a love affair." Then she spoke quickly, her words running together. "I cannot tell you how wonderful it was, after the years with Sam, years in which I had to please him, with his sallow skin, the folds in his face, and his sagging body, after that to hold a boy, his body so lean, his skin so smooth. Oh, what pleasure. Well, you know, I am sure you do, the wonders of a young man. I adore him; his soft hands rubbing my back would be enough for passion to fire my whole body. I dreamed of him every night. I still do, but his face seems further and further away. I cannot let that happen."

Far from being scandalized, Ilse found that she was excited "But … your husband?"

As they entered the apartment, Sara said, "Ah Ilse, he's so old! He began to watch what I did, depended on me for so much, and now there are no business ventures to occupy him either. If he had left me alone, maybe I could stand it. His whiskers annoyed me, his pigeon-toed walk. All his medicines. And, you know, he cannot even—" Ilse gasped and blushed, amazed at what Sara was about to say, but the older woman stopped short of being explicit, instead saying, "I just do not love him. Now, with Claude, I know what love is— he takes my breath away, his deep kisses thrill me, the wonder of it all. When he touched my body, my flesh burned—how can I compare that to my feelings for my husband, with his few wisps of hair and his little everything….?" Again she trailed off, but then she went on.

"It's not just that. Claude knows what *interests* me. He reads the latest novels; he even read me that French novel about women who love each other—Sam would never understand. I have to find Claude. We will live in a village; we will have a farm—"

"A farm!" Ilse burst into laughter. "I cannot imagine Claude on a farm!"

Sara grabbed Ilse's arm violently, "I don't want to go on if I cannot find Claude. I must find him. That's what keeps me going. I decided to change my life, and now I will do good things, for me, for Claude. I want to dress the most gangrened wounds, help those with the greatest suffering, and find him."

Sara continued, "I feel married—*really* married—to Claude. It is not about the ceremony. Look, here's a ring he gave me when he left for France. We were both crying. Of course his awful mother was hovering about; I actually think she was happy about the war, happy because it separated us. And so it has."

Ilse tried to imagine the scene, with the two women demanding Claude's attention. How were they dressed? Was Sara distressed and Mme. Bertram beaming victoriously? Did they speak to each other at all? Her son with a former milliner's assistant, a Slav, a Jewess—it must have driven the haughty French seamstress mad!

"Of course you are being wild and reckless," Ilse said, "and I want to help you. You must stay here with me; Georg will lodge in the barracks. You and I will take walks and cook together." Ilse could well imagine falling under Claude's spell, for she and Annette had idolized him as an *artiste*, a romantic poet, a young Werther.

Sara kissed Ilse's hands. "Everything is so clear to you. You know how repressed we Jews are, so afraid of any scandal, of giving any offense. I had to get away from Munich, you understand," she added. Outside, it was snowing again. Ilse wondered if the farmers would bring vegetables to the market the following week.

***

Sara, Heidi, and Ilse were lively. It was the weekend, so Sara wasn't applying tourniquets and Ilse was at home. Heidi brought a bottle of good Riesling—wine was not scarce. They cut and sliced vegetables, working quickly in the kitchen, soup for a few meals. After just a few weeks, they were close friends, Sara remarking, "Let's celebrate. We are free to think and act as young women. Who worries about bad form anymore? We don't need our fathers or husbands to pay for us now. We don't need to be leaving our visiting cards anywhere." She turned to Ilse. "I am so proud of you that you have taken a job and are independent." Then both Heidi and Sara drank a toast to Ilse.

Sara continued, her knife suspended, "Be careful, though, not to drive Georg away."

Ilse looked at Sara's deep dark eyes and was amused. That Sara, who had flouted the mores of society and fled her wealthy husband, should be alarmed for her was comically touching.

Ilse cut, cut, cut; her hands moved so swiftly that her friends barely saw the knife hit the board before it was in the air again. She took a gulp of the wine Heidi had brought, catching up with the other two, who were on a second glass.

Turning to Heidi, she said, "You almost look saucy." To Sara she said, "I am trying to support her in her clothing decisions."

"It's the Munich revolution," said Sara. "If you stick with us too long, you will be wild and mad, like the wild women of Bavaria! Lonely wives must keep up appearances; we must hug ourselves, for our men cannot do it now."

"Oh, Sara, do tell us, what do your men say?" her friends egged her on.

"My men, indeed!"

"I know you have suitors. You can't hide your late nights from me," Ilse said.

"Yes, I go out at night. I am not young like you, but my heart is young and restless, and I need a man to hug me. I really will go mad otherwise. I can't sleep, I can't think … I want someone to say I am a rose, sometimes a thorn, but always they would pick me and have me!"

"What do you love the most—kisses or hugs?" Ilse asked.

"The groin!" exclaimed Sara.

They got tipsier.

They left the soup simmering and Sara hugged Ilse tightly and squeezed her. "There was another reason I came here. Promise me this—if I have a child, you will take care of it! Promise me." She grasped Ilse tightly, not realizing how hard, and Ilse pushed her away.

"Be cautious," Heidi said. "It feels like nothing will ever be the same. Our values have changed. The damned war! But why shouldn't women seek love? It's completely natural," she mused.

Ilse frowned. "You can be cautious because you love your husband. He's your darling, and you are his. But what if that isn't the case? Then should a woman be condemned to chastity? No, I cannot believe that. Yet I don't condone adultery." Taking her wineglass, Ilse went to the main room, the parlor, mulling over this contradiction, but she couldn't think clearly. Heidi and Sara followed her.

Heidi said, "That's merely desire. You cannot call that flame love."

Drunkenly, Sara twisted Ilse's hair over her head. "You're hurting me, Sara. Stop." Sara seemed not to hear, only hiccupping and falling into Ilse's arms. Ilse cradled her in her lap and finger brushed her hair, wet from excitement.

"I wouldn't say you are promising drunkards," Heidi said.

Sara was spirited. "Who can judge—a deep kiss, the prelude to copulation? There are new ways of loving," Sara continued. "It's all the rage now. Come on, you two must at least be curious!"

Ilse thought, *it must be marvelous to be free like Sara, in a liaison with a young handsome Frenchman, then fleeing to the front to find him.*

"I'm thinking of my husband at the front," Heidi was crying quietly, drinking more wine.

"I am so ignorant," Ilse admitted.

Sara took her hand and started kissing her arm, making Ilse squirm, collapsing in ticklishness.

"That's enough, ladies!" Heidi said, trying to be mirthful.

Sara buried her head in Ilse's lap and then touched her in a way that made Ilse jump, orange in the face.

Sara didn't notice. "Here's the thing," she slurred. "I won't live much longer."

"Shhh! A demon is lurking in you," said Heidi.

"Heidi, you're the only one who has children," Ilse said, "so tell us—what's it like?"

"I never knew such love existed, the love I had for my baby, a child that needed me to feed him, take care of him, depended on me for everything. It's different than any other love. Well, you cannot tell what will happen or how your children turn out. Our boy is very modern, he's a free thinker, to our surprise. Every sacrifice we made was worthwhile to see him become a young man. I know he'll turn back to God."

Then Heidi wailed, "Now my dear son is in a battle zone, lying in a field bed, if he even has a bed. Maybe lying on his greatcoat in the mud, sleeping in a wild place. Must I sacrifice the child I love?"

"Could I be a mother?" Ilse asked. "I probably won't be any good at it."

"It will be completely natural," Heidi managed to say. "You will see, when the war is over, it will be easier. Your sister's children will play with yours, there will be peace between you, and the family outings will be special. A child's touch is so gentle, yet altogether intense."

Heidi went into the kitchen and poured the soup and began to sing—and then the three of them ate and sang:

Lieb Vaterland mags(magst) ruhig sein,
Wir wollen alle Mütter sein—
Treu steht und fest die Wacht am Rhein.[*]

"I won't forget this day," Heidi said. "I'm going now. No more wine, ladies! And you two better not ravish each other."

"We should give you some food to take, Heidi!" Ilse said, but she was too unbalanced to stand.

"We should," said Sara—and then looking up at Ilse, she added, "If I have a baby, will you really take care of it?"

Ilse was only half conscious. "Why, silly thing, of course I will."

Heidi left them both sleeping, with their skirts riding up a bit, more than a little disheveled.

---

[*] *"Die Wacht am Rhein"* as quoted in <u>No Man's Land</u>, edited Pete Ayrton, selection 'Hut 5B', Miroslav Krleža, tr. By Celia Hawkesworth p. 316.

17

February 1915

On her way home from the museum, Ilse searched for ingredients for *Glühwein*. She would make it for Sara, it would warm both of them, but it was hard to find such treats— going from shop to shop her toes and fingers felt frozen. She shuddered passing a matchbook peddler and bought matches. His face was disfigured, a casualty of the war. *When will it end?*

As she turned away she wept for Walther, who had dreaded violence, *how horrible if his corpse was not found, his body parts dispersed on French soil.* Of course he had to be buried at home, but how could that be if he was missing?

Like many Berliners, Ilse grieved that German men, simple farmers and workers, were killing mercilessly, urged on by the ambitions of the Kaiser, Austria's Emperor Franz Joseph, and the nobility, for a dispute that was now inexplicable. At the beginning, the pageantry had swept her along with the crowds, Germany was being threatened by her enemies, everyone had said that. Now as the death lists in the *Tageblatt* grew, the war became a curse on Germany.

Entering the apartment, she heard loud laughter—Georg's. This was not the formal way he had with strangers. Then she saw Sara's hands in his.

"I'm warming up her hands. They were frozen," he freed Sara's hands. "I can thaw yours too."

Ilse remained still, Sara mouthed words, and Georg glanced away. He tried to laugh, but Ilse knew the insincerity of the laugh he now affected. Everything she saw was strange, but Sara was happy, her cheeks pink, elated at Georg's attentions. Ilse mumbled, "What's going on?"

"*Privyet*, hello," Sara said, blowing Ilse a kiss. "We're having an elementary Russian lesson. Your husband is a fast learner. I'm showing him how to use his tongue to make certain Russian sounds."

"*Zdrastvui*, hello," Georg said, flashing cold, seemingly angry eyes on Ilse, a warning and perhaps a joke. His braided jacket was unbuttoned and half open, and Ilse saw he was fussing with an old, short pipe.

Failure, she thought. *I found God's love, but in the struggle I failed Georg. He might die on the front. I love him; I feel compassion for Sara, why do I make such a mess? I forgive his infidelities, but I'm jealous, too — how could he desire Sara, a close friend? He's charming her, so suggestive with his large hands working the pipe and restlessly drumming on the arms of the chair. How could he have an affair with her? Heidi was right: he is easy prey for women.*

Georg began to appear several times a week and fill his old pipe and sit in his accustomed chair as Sara gave him Russian lessons. Before he arrived in the evening, Sara took a leisurely bath, emerging with water dripping, humming Russian tunes. Sara was transformed once more into a dazzling charmer, her wide eyes bright and excited, and she took more care arranging her curls and looking at herself in a small silver mirror, wearing trinkets she had been buying recently. Sometimes she filled Georg's short pipe for him. In front of Ilse, she placed her hand on his shoulder, then jokingly on his chin, and giggled and hummed.

There were evenings when Georg tested out the stories for his journal, or complained bitterly about lost opportunities for victory. By turns, he was light hearted or morose. He insisted that if von Moltke hadn't argued with Conrad, the Eastern Front battles wouldn't have been so costly—tens of thousands dead and more than ten thousand irreplaceable horses lost. In a better mood, he spun out a tale about the proud General Bielenberg who rode with his scabbard and got stuck in his stirrup, his horse then carrying him a kilometer before rushing soldiers saved him.

Some days, he spoke of dead soldiers. "We peeled clothes off the dead, that was the slowest and worst part of battle, after a barrage, checking for wounds, for body parts. We removed packets of letters from soldiers' pockets, mostly letters for parents and wives." Georg's voice trembled.

Ilse would say, "You loved your men. God gave you that love. His way is not the way of the nations and the armies."

Another time, "The suffering that grips the heart from love is sharper than all other torture."

His fist would come down on the table, "That's no comfort."

Then he would get some beers and he and Sara would clink 'Za vas'.

Hours after he left, Ilse heard Sara tiptoe out. She suspected they were embracing in an apartment of one of Georg's friends, or squeezed in his officer's cot at barracks.

Then one day there was silence. Sara left for the front, with many exuberant kisses, her eyes brighter than ever, without remorse for the husband she deserted, for Ilse or Georg's sorrow, kissing "her dear, kind Ilse" three times on each cheek. She did not have to say how happy she was—she glowed, her brightness was alluring, even glamorous, and she suddenly spoke of being closer to Claude. She was free and somehow oblivious to any pain or distress she might have caused.

After she left, Georg rarely came from the officers' mess except to hand over part of his wages when, with cold eyes, he greeted Ilse's perplexed look. He never mentioned Sara, but after she left he became restless, unable to contain bursts of anger. Ilse supposed it galled him that Sara was at the front, while he was a city dweller, strolling in Berlin, an angry man.

***

A senior museum staff member, who had spent years in Italy, took

Ilse under his wing and introduced her to collectors. Although the Arts Academy would not favor a Jew, even a curator, with membership, it turned to him for advice and invited him to meetings and ceremonies. Members asked him for appraisals and invited him to concerts. Connoisseurs who sought him out included families hoarding gold during the war. Collectors trusted his discretion. In the summer of 1914, he had advised his German clients to bring their gold back to Germany, and they were indebted to him. Not yet affected by the war, the wealthy Wolff heirs, the Baron of Oldenburg, and even the King of Italy continued to collect and bid at auctions with his help.

He placed paintings and objects of lesser known Renaissance artists in Ilse's care; taught her how to handle paintings, note their condition and any earlier restorations and check the reverses for the artist's graffiti and the museum's labels. She enjoyed private jokes with the museum staff, and together they read catalogue entries and "gambled" pfennige, guessing at prices in upcoming auctions and who the bidders might be. She found out that the museum world was full of its own secrets and intrigues; there was so much for her to understand. She read old catalogues and traced the provenance of art works. She followed recommendations made by Georg's parents and borrowed their books on Pisanello and di Matteo. After a few weeks, Georg returned home, and they lived in the apartment like distant friends.

The nation was gripped with fervor for German art. During the first month of the war, not only was East Prussia saved, but the German part of Alsace Lorraine was successfully defended from French invaders. Works of art that had languished were suddenly considered representative of the German character and brought out of seclusion. Matthias Grünewald's famous altarpiece, which had been controlled by Germany since 1871 remained in the Reich. ** The altarpiece, a symbol of German genius, was brought to Munich, and displayed there.

Seeing the altarpiece for the first time, art historians like Georg's parents reevaluated famous German painters—Grünewald, Schongauer, and Dürer—and many now thought the altarpiece a national treasure,

---

** The Franco-Prussian War 1870-1871

the paragon of German art, with its expressive depiction of agony and horror.

With Sara gone, Georg's parents again invited Ilse and Georg to join them for Sunday dinners. "We have just come back from viewing the altarpiece—exquisite!" Georg's father said one afternoon. "The iconography is uncanny. Maybe one day you two will go with us to see it."

"What a wonderful suggestion!" said Georg's mother, Lottie, the peacemaker. "We must all go while Georg is home."

"Yes," Ilse said, then, "You've given me a wonderful idea. I can curate an exhibit to stimulate national feeling here on the home front. The Gemäldegalerie may have all I need. I'm drawn to the Northern Renaissance style. Dürer's images of Christ shattered my preconceptions about Christian art. Instead of being meek and plaintive, Dürer's figures are strong and muscular, bearing swords and traveling on vultures. In school, I spent hours copying them."

Georg's father sat back and said, "A wonderful idea. You always impress me, young lady. No sooner does one project end than you are tearing off on another."

Ilse turned to Georg. "Would you go to the museum to see fifteenth-century art, Dürer's self-portraits, for instance?"

"As usual, darling, your ideas are sound," he replied stiffly in his fine baritone.

In his parents' company, Georg enjoyed being with Ilse. She was always thinking ahead, planning, reading, and coming up with projects. Had there been no war, had Sara not come to Berlin, they might easily go back to how things were. He thought *Ilse's the finest person I know*, and he regretted his early infidelities. He was ashamed that he had betrayed Ilse. *I'm no knightly hero,* he thought, *will our marriage ever go back to the way it was?*

After dinner, Werther turned to Ilse. "Here are some books which may give you ideas for an exhibit. We all respect your fierce ambition." He emphasized the word *all*.

When Georg arrived home the next evening, slightly drunk after an officer's party, the desk was covered with tomes on Dürer. Ilse had been feverishly examining the master's self-portraits, from a modest drawing when Dürer was only thirteen years old to a final masterpiece showing the artist in magnificent furs. Georg's eye fell on a drawing that Dürer had made of himself and his wife, Agnes.

"Remind me—why am I looking at this?" asked Georg, lighting a cigarette for her and smoking it until she took it. Then he picked up his pipe and added tobacco to it, sitting in his favorite chair, where Sara had lit his pipe. He knew Dürer's portraits but could only vaguely recall what Ilse was doing.

"Don't you think this would be a marvelous exhibit?" She was eager, full of serious intent, flicking ashes into the ashtray with her thumb, though she was hardly smoking.

"You've chosen Dürer for your subject, very wise," he said, "but at best you will only be able to obtain poor copies of these. You will spend months in polite letter writing, but the Albertina and the Kunsthalle most likely won't lend their paintings and drawings; too dangerous to transport now."

What an idiot I am, he thought. *I should let her pursue this. Why should I frustrate her? Why not let her do what she wants?*

Despite himself, he continued, "Ilse, let's go over Dürer's other work. Maybe the woodcuts will be more promising, since prints can usually be located more easily, and there are already woodcut prints in the Gemäldegalerie. Perhaps my father would even lend the museum prints from his collection. Art dealers whose business is languishing now may also want the free publicity."

They set to work together. Watching her exuberance, he recalled the thrill he had felt when first studying ancient coins. She took notice of a subtle change in his manner toward her; while he was no longer affectionate, he genuinely respected her ambition, admired her fierce look.

"My idea is that you should show Dürer's continuity with German tradition, especially now," he said after they had searched for a while. "So I would look to an early series of prints that are rooted in German art, and not pursue his later portraits or paintings. In his mature paintings Dürer was very influenced by the Venetians. There's a subject my parents can talk about for hours—the rapport between European Renaissance art in the North and South."

"Ah! You're such a Renaissance man, and so very smart!" Ilse was only half teasing. "I remember how you and Stephen Walsh talked until the morning about the classics. I wonder if Walsh's poems have been published. Such an interesting man. Venice was full of happy adventures."

"Yes, it was a sweet time, and Walsh was a good fellow to drink with, that American Casanova. I see he made an impression. Maybe I will adopt his persona. What do you think? I might make a good minstrel too," he joked. "I would become one if it appealed to you. Meanwhile, our task is to find something in early Dürer, something that will be accessible to viewers. Before the war, the Kaiser, the public, they came to view Casper David Friedrich paintings. The Kaiser's penchant for Böcklin is well known. People want to see art that reflects our national style. Starting with early Dürer is a good idea. Your exhibit should reveal his imagination."

Taking Georg's advice, she set about looking at prints in the museum the very next day. She began with Dürer's prints of the *Man of Sorrows*, admiring the silvertone in the early drawing and the way Christ was shown looking boldly at the viewer. She asked Georg what he thought.

"Showing only suffering is inappropriate now; we are mired in war, and victory eludes us. Do not frighten mothers and wives who might see their loved ones in His face. Try to find drawings with a suggestion of a noble war and redemption. I promise you among Dürer's work there are cycles that will be suitable."

She wanted to lash out at him, but she also needed his help. He understood the art world, while she was a novice. His parents were respected art historians, and she would need their contacts.

The next day, she tried again. "For the exhibit, I will assemble the illustrations from Dürer's woodcuts, which followed the tradition of popular devotional art. I chose the Apocalypse cycle, because it deals with redemption. The exhibit can also cover bibles printed in the same period."

"Stupefying!" he said enthusiastically. "I was just thinking that the devotional Apocalypse cycle would make the best exhibit."

He seemed sincere, but she didn't know if he had come to this idea at the same time or was just agreeing to keep peace. There was pain and suffering in the Apocalypse cycle, but she thought that its themes of redemption and victory over the Antichrist were just as prominent. She asked, "The series imagines war magnificently, and people will relate to it. Do you agree that the violent battle with Antichrist, the cosmic war, is an appropriate subject for this warlike time?"

Georg had not touched Ilse in weeks, but at this moment, he spontaneously put his arms around her and kissed her. To his surprise, she kissed him back, even opening her mouth slightly, though it seemed more in surprise than desire.

Then she disengaged herself. "The whole cycle—imagine all fifteen illustrations on display! If I also obtain the frontispiece, it will be a handsome exhibit. I will include the text underneath in German and Latin, so that viewers can understand Dürer's intent."

The war was everywhere, in every aspect of life—he had waited a long time to hear his fair-skinned wife finally understand about the violence of war, and now her understanding of the war was deepening. There were newsreels which showed the war, although they omitted images he had seen too often, empty eye sockets, bones protruding from bodies, blasted pectorals— he hoped she would never see these. Naive, slim, neat Ilse.

He restrained himself from embracing her. Why shouldn't she seek advancement and the exhibit be a success? If it were, he would be proud of her.

"It's interesting how Dürer portrays peasants and ordinary people," he said to her. "Look at the second illustration in the cycle, and you'll see Dürer's fondness for the simple people. Look here, in the martyrdom of John the Evangelist, how the onlookers are sympathetic innocents.

This follows the German Gothic tradition, while literally referring back to the Gospel."

The Martyrdom of Saint John, The Apocalypse, Albrecht Dürer

Ilse said, "There is such revolutionary fervor, such thunder and lightning, almost a bellowing in Dürer's depiction."

He said approvingly. "When you show the similarity with other printed German bibles, you can also show the difference with earlier manuscripts, where illuminators drew calm countenances. Now show me how you will caption one of these prints, if you please, Frau Curator."

"Let me read you what I wrote for Revelation 10 and Dürer's woodcut, beginning with the verse itself: 'And I saw another mighty angel come down from heaven, clothed with a cloud: and a rainbow was upon his head, and his face was as it were the sun, and his feet as pillars of fire: "'And he had in his hand a little book open: and he set his right foot upon the sea, and his left foot on the earth.'" (Rev. 10:1–2, KJV)

"This is so literal, the angel drawn without a body," she continued, reading her handwriting from a card. "Dürer's carving mirrors the actual words spoken by Saint John: 'And the voice which I heard from heaven spake unto me again, and said, Go and take the little book which is open in the hand of the angel which standeth upon the sea and upon the earth. And I went unto the angel, and said unto him, Give me the little book. And he said unto me, Take it and eat it up.' (Rev. 10:9 KJV)

"It's a marvelous woodcut with John devouring the pages, the altar suspended on high, and the contrasting of supernatural with natural, of heaven and earth."

Saint John Devouring the Book, The Apocalypse, Albrecht Dürer

Georg was proud of her, "I hope you will also place your text clearly on the side of the prints. This is how I would do it." He wrote the following on a blank card:

Upper Scene: The ark, the heavenly altar, praying angels

Center: The angel with pillars of fire at his feet

Lower scene: John the Evangelist ingesting the book (God's Word/ John's prophesy) — in foreground Dürer's rendering of grasses and reeds

"I think you need to make it clear what is depicted as each woodcut includes several images and the woodcuts are very detailed. Let me see what you will write about the final woodcut, which portrays the New Jerusalem. It's one of my favorites."

"Yes, yes," she said, "but first let's have a beer."

Casually, as if there had never been a betrayal, they drank and smoked and smiled. Ilse hummed, and Georg wondered if they would ever dance quietly in the dark again.

After a while, Ilse said, "Let me take a look at that print. Yes, I will try to follow your example and highlight the different events. Let's see: In the upper scene an angel, ready to usher in the faithful, shows Saint John the New Jerusalem. In the imagery of the lower scene the angel carries the heavy keys to hell while chaining Satan."

The Angel with the Key to the Bottomless Pit,
The Apocalypse, Albrecht Dürer

"Don't forget to note how the New Jerusalem is a neat German town," Georg said.

"I will indeed, my Herr Professor!" she said with mock seriousness. She was cheerful; would Georg dance with her? Would it be that night?

She realized a small catalogue with selections from Revelation would be needed, which might cause problems in the department. Funds were limited so she would have to manage the situation carefully, soliciting donors tactfully. There might be tension as other curators sought out the same philanthropists—she would have to risk that.

Her new position was tenuous at best. She had not been accepted as an equal by several elderly curators, the remnant of the staff after the younger professors left for the front. While she was engrossed thinking of donors, Georg played lightly with her curls. He was smiling, and she cast her eyes down.

Why have I pushed her away? How many wasted weeks! Georg thought. *She is a stranger to me, and perhaps she doesn't want intimacy with me after all. Of course she wouldn't tell me if I revolted her.* He was angry with himself and he wanted her to show a grand generosity.

She broke the silence. "Imagine, if we are successful, we will be able to show Dürer's later work after the war is won."

"Or perhaps, I would wish, the national spirit will wane after the war," Georg asked.

"You make nationalism sound bitter and distasteful."

"And so it is. I think the combination of nationalism and industry will destroy Germany, certainly Germany as we know it. But the art created in Germany will outlive the devastation of this war; the killing, the maiming, the sickness that war brings. Men cannot destroy the ideal and sublime. Dürer conveyed the national spirit, undoubtedly, at the same time as the Italians conveyed the individual human spirit. Dürer's handling of his subjects is dynamic and hundreds of years from now, his art will still be admired."

By now, with the beer, Georg was also in a good mood. "It's odd, isn't it," he said, "that we two Jewish pariahs can sit here and studiously discuss Christian art. I know, Ilse, you truly feel the spirit. I wish I could. Conversion was a stepping stone, a convenience, for me. I lack your faith."

She looked at him, so awkward at this moment, trying to convey something and to please her, yet unable to express himself. Perhaps he was no longer enjoying evenings in the cafés, the officers' parties. She wanted to say something to help him, so that he would understand that she still loved him, admired him, that she found him attractive. For a second, she saw herself as a childless old crone, stooped, looking at Grünewald's altarpiece, and there was Georg and a lovely woman, herself, and he was lifting a child up on his shoulders. She snapped awake and saw that he was staring at her. He was hoping for something, some word, so she smiled; she raised her head and smiled directly at him, then she ran her fingers through his hair.

***

The days and weeks raced by. It was April, a season of new promise, migrating birds, blossoms opening, and yet war weariness continued after a winter of hunger. Now Georg was returning to the Eastern Front, childless. Ilse hid her despair that she was not pregnant.

Artillery regiments were concentrated on the Eastern Front, including troops being shifted from France— Georg hoped he would finally own the Iron Cross. He was reporting to the Eleventh Army, which would crush the Russians. There was a rumor that the troops would then be transferred to France for a final victory there. By the end of the year the war would be over, the slaughter would end and, with peace, farming would flourish again, food would be plentiful, he and Ilse would start a family.

His last week home, they danced every night and lovingly took turns making breakfast for each other, eggs, if there were any, and whatever bruised fruit they found in the market. Ilse put some spring flowers, the very first, in an enormous vase.

"I will miss you so," he said.

"Pfoo." She tried to be cheerful. "You have been missing your regiment; now you will miss me. Soon you'll be home again!"

They drank two bottles of wine the night before Georg left and slept little. At dawn, it took some arranging to close Georg's thirty-kilogram knapsack, and hugging was awkward. As they left for the station, their neighbor Frau Gantz was watering her patio flowers and called out, "Auf Wiedersehen, Gott schütze Sie." Georg stole a last look at the manicured lawn around their building, the blooming clusters of yellow and salmon-colored tulips and the apple trees, which he imagined leafing and budding in May. In the horse-drawn cab, he looked out the rectangular window, and he was still peering out when they arrived in front of the station with its domed hall, full of somber people.

Ilse had tears in her eyes.

"Imagine this is a grand cathedral," Georg said, smiling weakly to comfort her, "pray that soon you will be greeting me, returning home."

On the platform there was chaos, parents kissing their sons goodbye—the two once arrogant men from the optical factory were among the new recruits. Georg dreaded thinking of these young men at the front, and he turned away from them, so very young, so soon to be thrust into action, carrying Mauser rifles, rushing forward, killing or being killed.

Tired workers were cleaning the eastbound train, loading water and coal as more soldiers and families arrived. Ilse's heart pounded in the commotion. She batted away thoughts of Sara, that wicked woman, of whom they had not once spoken. *All has been well*, she thought. She let go all ideas of treachery. *He'll be gone, but he'll write to me and return to me.*

"Why such a deep frown?" he asked. "Farewell and no sweet smile?"

She was sorry he had noticed. They shared a last long kiss, and then his train was ready. The cars were attached, and he turned, threw his knapsack onto the train, and stepped up, then kissed her hand from the window.

Will I see him again? Will he return safely? With a heavy heart, Ilse took the omnibus home. *Do these other passengers feel so much grief?*

Heidi visited later, hugging her tightly, and Frau Gantz made ersatz chops for dinner. That night, a messenger brought a note from Georg's parents, inviting Ilse to Sunday lunch. They were certainly making an effort. How sad that her marriage with Georg had caused both families grief and ruptured Moshe's ties with his sister Lottie.

Why couldn't she get it right? She tried and tried. She was like a child solving problems by numbers, but it never came out right. She believed the right things; she was convinced of that.

Leon had been writing weekly, and Ilse now read a new letter about Annette's family: *"What an industrious fellow Martin is. Annette may be pregnant again. Business is slow, but Martin has closed some of the presses and sold equipment while the main printing press limps along. He's very devoted to Annette and his sons.*

The military industrialists are getting richer, comfortable, with full bellies... It is not enough to demonstrate against capitalists. I have to worm my way into their operations. I am going to work for AEG. Soldiers are dying while the men running these companies are profiting.

At home, the sadness about Walther, and grief at the inability to bury him, lingers. Sometimes Papa despairs, and now it is Mama who keeps up the traditions, and Martin walks Papa to the synagogue.

Although they don't admit it, Mama and Papa are proud of the exhibit you curated. I read them the reviews in the newspaper. Good work!"

18

August 5, 1915

My Darling Ilse,

Warsaw is ours!

We have made up for time lost during the harsh winter. Sometimes, amidst all the rain and muck, there are quiet evenings like this one—there will be no shooting and no blasts here, nothing but peaceful snoring all around. Except for the sentries, everyone will get a good night's rest.

In a few days I will snoop around for merchants who sell old maps of this area in the 1600's and 1700's, and, of course, also for groats, denarii, ducats minted then or even before. I hope to bring home a fine map of the Kingdom of Poland and Duchy of Lithuania at the height of their power. I have written some pieces on our military administration, but mostly I write about the people, a mishmash, Poles, Russians, Jews. There are pictures of saints everywhere and boastful church buildings built by the Czarist regime look strangely out of place amidst the poverty here. I am sending you an illustration of the wooden houses here and the droshkies, little one horse carriages.*

This whole area is scarred by the war. Retreating, the Russian Army incinerated barns, fields, and crops. The ramshackle huts have cracks and thatched roofs, unlike the neat farms of our homeland. The manors of the

---

* Dehmel, Richard, <u>Zwischen Volk und Menschheit, Kriegstagebuch</u>

nobility were burned to the ground. Some artisans' tools, knives, rusted sharpening instruments were left behind, women's torn shawls, children's socks. In this confusion, bandits live in the thick forests, plundering and poaching at night, sneaking into abandoned villages, looting anything they can find. They butcher any stray animal, a goat, a cow, a dog. There's more danger here from such bandits, nearly savages, than from the enemy soldiers.

A year ago our people abandoned their homes in East Prussia. Terrible as that ordeal was, it was not as horrific as the displacements here. As our troops advanced, residents in border areas, like Bjekow, were evacuated by the Russian army, mostly Jews. Hundreds of thousands,[**] not knowing where to go, have pushed their cartloads of junk into Russia's interior cities.[***] The Jews and peasants who eluded deportation live in outlying villages in tattered clothes or torn sheepskins without any protection. In Warsaw Jewish refugees wander desperately seeking food and shelter. Former doctors, lawyers, farmers, try to find work or beg to survive.

Refugees fit for work are forced into labor camps by any army that finds them.

In Bjekow, we learned that the peasants and Jews in this village were driven out by the Russian Army in a blizzard—old people, women, and children. Jews either found food or perished on the road. They marched for days, beaten mercilessly by Cossacks' whips. We saw flayed corpses of women protecting their children's bodies on the road.

Last week, something unusual happened. It would have been just another dreary night passed in whistling and singing if the kitchen cart had come on time. Some of us left camp to search for food and blankets, as nights are so damp. We had plenty to drink, but no meat, which had been promised for days. A hungry pack, we set out to scavenge, our throats burning with vodka.

Desperately, we searched in the mosses—we challenged one another to eat thistles. We would have eaten ants on a dare. We cursed this blasted land, the poor Slavs who live here and the retreating Russians who burned everything. We cursed the wild forest, its spectral remnants, stumps where

---

[**] Manley, Rebecca in <u>To the Tashkent Station</u>, writes that from 1915-1917 over three million people were displaced in the Russian Empire.

[***] Gatrell, Peter, <u>A Whole Empire Walking</u>, chaps. 4 and 7, also p. 84.

trees were felled for firewood. We kept to the edge of the forest, to avoid bandits. Emil shot drunkenly at shadows.

Frustrated and gripped by a sweaty anger, we came upon three Jews huddled together, like beasts. Two bedraggled youths were holding a shriveled old man who was either kneeling or falling. The old man was wearing a torn black coat, spattered with mud, his face hidden by a fur hat, tilted at a crazy angle. One of the soldiers grabbed switches, just to make them dance and amuse us, as a joke. Then the old man crumpled, hardly bled, and died, dark-brown spots oozing from his body.

Old refugee

The episode lasted seconds, and our men laughed. They did not realize the old man had died. Suddenly, they heard the kitchen wagon and ran for the stew.

A sorrowful sound rooted me and Dietrich to the spot. The taller boy was howling into his cupped hands. He was not more than fifteen or sixteen years old. Just a reed of a boy, laying the not-yet-stiff, black-coated figure on the ground. Zayde Isaac, Grandfather, he wept—I could hear him and understand him now—and he knew we were watching him, but he did not flinch. He was not afraid of us. He was filthy, scrawny, and yet he moved with grace and nobility. We were two armed soldiers, his fate in our hands, and yet this boy stared us down with intense green eyes.

This strange, fair boy is remarkable in this land of rain, mud, and vermin. The Russian Army, now a woeful group, also starving, portrays Jews as spies, as devils and abuses them. You know your father's stories—a Jewish life is worth nothing in this miserable place, where villages are hardly deserving of a name. How the Jews here sustained life, even maintaining the rituals of cleanliness and purity, is hard to understand. Somehow they still kept their faith and held fast to their sacred Torah scrolls.

Jewish refugees near Lublin praying in a field

I ordered this boy and the other youngster, who had hidden behind a tree, to follow us back to camp. But the fair boy, covered with sores and boils, refused.

He began digging his zayde's grave with his hands.

Dietrich said, "Let's leave now before the boys make trouble."

I agreed with Dietrich, but I could not leave them there. This strange, fair boy was maddening; emaciated yet tall, stubbornly digging a deep pit. After he clawed awhile, his hands bled and, as if he were a commander in the army, he ordered the other boy to continue the digging.

That younger emaciated boy followed our every movement and word, obeyed without saying a word.

"Why doesn't this boy speak?" we asked the fair boy, who shrugged.

The boys were manacled, held in our "prison", a closet, to be sent to a labor camp next morning. Yet somehow at night the younger boy ran away. The guard is an old soldier, a former schoolteacher, and he's like a father to many of us. A brave soldier, he was awarded the Iron Cross in 1870. Probably a prank by a drunken soldier. The boy seemed a half-wit who wouldn't survive hard labor. He will be caught in the forest by one side or the other. The fair young man doesn't want to flee and we unbound him; he wants protection and safety with us, and is willing to work hard.

He lives in our barracks now and eats with us. He eats very little, though he drinks like a military veteran. Of drink, there is no shortage. We have shorn his fair forelocks, and the men joke because he's so blond. He told us in Yiddish that he and the old man and other boy had been living off flowers and weeds and mushrooms, scrounging but not daring to enter the forest. His zayde was dying; he had suffered too much. It was better he was now in Olam Haba'ah, the world to come. We call him Osip, or Josif, and sometimes Yossele. He has become our mascot, along with the camp dogs, and some of the men say they'll teach him proper German. He's very confident, knows he's smart, and during this lull in fighting I'll educate him. He never mourns his grandfather, his family or the other boy but is cheerful. He sleeps on a straw bed, as we're short of beds, pillows, and blankets.

I even imagine making a fine soldier of him! When fully healed of sores, I know his features will be like those of a Greek warrior, classic and heroic.

I am proud that our soldiers see that there are village Jews who are beautiful and I want this unfortunate yet extraordinary boy to be accepted in our midst, and will try to civilize him. I will treat him like a son. I feel some relief from the trials of the last few months in helping him. Would you say that this is a good deed? Maybe this letter will still reach you before my next leave. I'll have so much to tell you about Josif then.

I am thinking of our future, when we will be together, and wish it were tomorrow. I miss you terribly.

I send a kiss, which I would rather give in person!

Your Georg

19

August 1915

In July Frau Gantz's son was killed in the Argonne Forest.

To forget the pain and turmoil, Ilse often walked in a small, sunflower field near her apartment. The sunflowers were bright, their heads nodding beautifully. Standing there on a hot summer day, the sky a luscious blue, Ilse prayed for calm and order. Like many of her neighbors, she wore black; in her heart she knew Walther was dead.

Drawing near her building, still thinking of the resplendent flowers, Ilse saw a ragamuffin, maybe fourteen years old, sitting on the stone step. She reached to give him a few pfennings.

"I'm from the post," he said, handing her a telegram, pocketing her pfennings, and running off before she firmly grasped the flimsy piece of paper.

She was shaking as she ripped the telegram open. Was it a notification about Georg? She started making out words: Cologne, hospital, Sara. The telegram wasn't about Georg at all, but had come from the Western Front. So Georg must be safe, safe. Of course, she knew he was safe. If she had thought about it, a death notice would be delivered by soldiers, not a scrappy boy, probably filling in for his father. How young he was too.

Light-headed, still shaking, she sat down. For an instant, she had believed Georg was dead because she was frightened like all her neighbors. In the street, people froze if they saw soldiers walking in pairs, the bearers of ill tidings. How could she have let herself believe something so terrible? She was in a hurry to read the telegram and shrugged off probing her feelings. She read the words again:

"Cologne Hospital. Friend Sara Liebermann. No family. Gave birth. Please come to hospital. Near train station. Take baby boy to Berlin, to Georg Eddings, his father. Sister Brigitte, Head Nurse."

She read the telegram again. "Sara … Georg?" She rolled her head down to her knees. She was relieved that Georg was safe, but fatigued by the now-certain knowledge and shame that Sara and Georg betrayed her. She had suspected and not done anything about it. Sara's special showers and baths, even in frigid water, her preparations before she went on her night walks; of course she wasn't meeting strangers. Ilse had realized this then; a neighbor would have gossiped if Sara had been walking the streets alone. She was meeting Georg; she prepared her toilette as she had in Starnberg, to be attractive, to be held and admired, to be whispered to, and even told comforting lies. Perhaps Georg had been waiting near the building those nights. Ilse had chosen the simplest path, not to ask questions, not to know.

Only three years before, how merry they had been. Claude danced with her at the Liebermanns' party. Sara enveloped her in friendship, Walther was engaged to Leah, and her parents were devoted to each other. Sara was the older, sophisticated woman, so Ilse had thought. Yet even in the English Garden, she should have recognized that Sara wasn't perfect. She wasn't independent or educated. She had been poor, a manual laborer, and she learned how to use people. Her husband provided protection, and thereafter Sara intuited who would love her, worship her, and protect her.

What have you done, Sara'le? Ilse thought, with a sudden tenderness for her absent, irrational friend. "You were mad to think of finding Claude, but you and Georg? Oh Sara'le, how foolish you were. I should have protected you; I saw you were confused." Ilse spoke as if Sara were beside her. She continued talking to her absent friend. "While I was busy with the exhibit, the donors, Wolfflin's lectures, you were pleasuring Georg."

Ilse tried to sleep but started calculating January to August. It was clear—those late nights, when Georg was supposedly in barracks, Sara was meeting him. Ilse tossed for a few hours, then gave it up and wrote to Georg. He probably wouldn't get her letter for weeks.

It's a sign, she wrote. *I am going to Cologne. When you come on leave, you will see your son. We'll hold him, and we will love him.*

She was wet from cold perspiration, and her teeth were chattering. *Am I ill?* But no, she thought, she felt strange but not ill. She, Georg, and Sara were bound together, and she believed that this was her chance to be useful, the holy journey. This was the child for whom Georg had longed.

It was a time for gentleness. Sara was back in her life, and she had loved Sara. She must have been at fault if both Georg and Sara betrayed her. It was not all their doing; Georg had wanted a child, and Sara desperately needed love, even the pretense of love. Ilse had ignored the pleading in their eyes. With her ambition, her insensitivity, she now felt, she had been as responsible for their affair as they were. Ilse hadn't wanted to think about it. She rubbed her lips until they were raw, unaware that spots of blood were falling on the writing paper.

She thought back, back. She remembered the family bitterness, the untraditional wedding, but also the exciting trip to Venice. What was it Walsh had said? The wild fragrance certain women had, and how he always sensed when a desirable woman would lay her cape in the mud for him. She had laughed at his witticisms during the festival until Georg had appeared at her side. The two young men had recited the epigrams of Catullus, she remembered, and they had whispered—they were quite drunk—about women, about bacchantes, about seduction.

Even before that, she remembered Sara entering Sam's suite in Starnberg as a supplicant, not a wife, and she understood now the extremes to which Sara would go, humbling herself, to be protected. Sam's attention wasn't enough because he was old and preoccupied. When Claude, young and handsome, kissed her hand in the English Garden, Sara discovered love.

In the morning, Ilse set out for the train station, only to learn that the next three days' trains were reserved for soldiers. She was too nervous to stay at home and worked feverishly at the museum. She had no idea about babies and worried she would not know what to do. Heidi, ever helpful and practical, organized clothes, blankets, help from the church.

"Don't worry," Heidi said. "I'll help you. It will come to you naturally."

Finally, Ilse was in the train station with a ticket to Cologne. All around were glum soldiers, mothers holding babies, grandparents holding toddlers. For them, the train was departing too soon, its tender already filled with coal. After they found compartments and flung down their knapsacks, the soldiers rushed to the windows and held on to the fingers of their wives and children.

As the train pulled out of the station, the soldiers brooded, some looking out the compartment window, some with cigarettes hanging from their mouths. Ilse reached over and offered a young man a sandwich. *This could have been Georg,* she thought.

By noon, as their train rolled toward Cologne, the young man asked her when and where her husband died. Ilse said, "My husband is in the east, my brother was missing early in the war. It's for him I am mourning."

The young man bit his lip. "I expect I won't come back," he said. "Three of my school friends are here. We don't want to fight. Our parents, our teachers, they promised us the war would be over, and now we are sent to die. Oh, I am sorry," he said, seeing her reaction. "I did not mean to cause you pain. Forgive me. My name is Karl. Are you visiting relatives?" he asked, by way of apology.

"Pleased, I'm Ilse. A friend of mine is in the hospital at Cologne. She was a nurse with the Red Cross, but I am not sure what happened to her." She stifled her pain to answer him.

The soldiers sang:

Es ist bestimmt in Gottes Rath,
(daß man was man am liebsten hat)
Muß mieden(scheiden) …
It is certain in God's wisdom,

that from our dearest loved one
we must part.[*]

As she listened to the song, and the train streaked across Germany, Ilse remembered resting her shoulder on Georg's, and how gently he stroked her abdomen, believing she would get pregnant.

She and Karl smoked and he told her about his fiancée, his love for her, and his fear. "We wanted to get married before I left, we wanted to start a family, but her parents wouldn't consent. Always their reason was that the war will end quickly. Older boys from my school have been killed. They couldn't wait to sign up and were great heroes a year ago. Two of them are dead, their limbs recovered and buried in mass graves. Their bones will never be brought back to Germany."

After they talked some more Karl dozed off, the young fuzz on his face so endearing.

She thought of the thousands more young soldiers like Karl, someone's son, someone's fiancé or husband, who would die if the war continued. It should have made sense, but it didn't.

How much has happened, she thought, *since the war began*. Walther was probably dead; Sara fled Munich; Georg fathered a baby. Annette and Martin had two boys, the joy of her parents. All the while, young German men left school to kill or be killed themselves.

She slept fitfully, hallucinating that Georg and Sara were coupled, intertwined next to her, rubbing against her.

At dawn, the train whistled by a beautiful pine forest, and then the train reached Cologne.

"Cologne, next stop, Cologne, only passengers with special permits allowed further," the conductor shouted.

Karl helped her with her suitcase, and she wrote her address for him. "I know you will return home to your fiancée. Please write me about your wedding. God bless you," she said as they shook hands.

***

---

[*] · Printed with permission of Lieder.net, translated by John H. Campbell.

The hospital was indeed near the depot, and she walked past the twin-spired Gothic cathedral, making a mental note of its location. *I'll go there tomorrow*, Ilse thought as she entered the hospital.

Sister Brigitte was grateful she had come and spoke as they walked. "You're probably tired from the trip. Your friend is in another building—I hope you don't mind following me, it's a bit of a distance. Our patients are debilitated, and your friend is very ill. Please put on these gloves and a mask. Minor germs could kill some of these patients."

"Thank you, Sister," Ilse said. Maimed and dying soldiers filled the corridors. Some of the wounded spoke French; war prisoners, she realized.

Sara was in a civilian ward, and as they walked, Sister Brigitte said, "I understand your friend was with a medical team. Their ambulance was hit and exploded. Your friend survived with serious burns."

There was a strong smell of antiseptic throughout the ward, where a young girl, hostile and gaunt, was scrubbing the floor. Despite the antiseptic, there was a putrid odor that grew stronger as they neared Sara's bed.

"It's the wound," the sister said as Ilse coughed into a handkerchief. The girl, it occurred to Ilse, was French, a war slave. She wore a mask, but her eyes were frightening—Ilse had never seen a look of such utter hatred.

Sara was facing the wall, her face bandaged. Her blanket had fallen off, or maybe she had pulled it off, and a purple crust could be seen on her hip and fingers.

Sister Brigitte said, "You have a guest, the friend you told me about."

"My friends hate me," Sara said, in the same voice Ilse remembered.

"Such thoughts prevent your mending," replied Sister Brigitte kindly. "It would be better not to hide your face from us."

"I am slipping, falling. Is that you, Ilse?" she asked. "Don't look at my face," she pleaded.

For a while, no one said anything. Then Ilse asked, "Shall I cover you with your blanket?" and gently she folded the blanket over Sara.

"I was down, down a dark, slimy tunnel," Sara moaned, and her chest heaved.

Quite suddenly, she became delirious, crying out in half German, half Russian: "Who are you? My sister, that is, you're a sister, but I don't have a sister. Are you Brigitte? *Hilf mir, veytik,* help me, my pain." She thrashed, threw her blanket off again, and pulled her hair, still facing the wall, hissing, "*Ukhodi,* get away, *Goryashchiy ogon, brennt,* burning fire." Within a second, she turned to Ilse and grabbed her hand, screaming, "*Pomogi mne,* help me!"

Then she lay still, exhausted. She was wet from fever and struggling. Ilse waited, but Sara was depleted, and her chest barely moved.

A civilian nurse came in and asked Ilse if she had a place to stay. "I hope you aren't eager to see the boy right now," she said.

"The boy." Ilse remembered, Georg's child. Was it possible? It was some dream; the war had confused everything.

"He's staying with a wet nurse, but she will bring him here tomorrow morning."

As they walked back, Ilse heard the piercing screams of a man removing bandages from his head; over and over he shouted, "Kill me, kill me." Another man, somewhere in the ward, began screaming, "It's the hole in his head. It's opening again, I'll stop him, for good." This second man moved in his bed, ready, it seemed, to pounce on the man with the bandaged head, but as he attempted to leap, he fell, and Ilse recoiled. His legless torso writhed on the floor, and the nurse, who was of average size, assisted him from behind, so that with the power of his strong hands, he lunged back into his bed.

Sister Brigitte pinned the first man to his bed while another nurse administered an injection. Then the two nurses bandaged the head wound, but before they started, Ilse saw the festering hole on the side of his head. She grabbed a towel and retched. The nurses, however, did everything calmly for the wounded soldier.

Afterward, Ilse asked, "Can he recover from such a wound?"

"Hard to tell," Sister Brigitte said. "I thought he would die when he came here; that was several weeks ago, but his condition hasn't changed.

We pray for him. Please put him in your prayers too. When he's not sedated, he's in terrible pain."

"And if he recovers, will his torment be over?"

"He might not recover his faculties; he might not be able to perform simple functions. There is so much we do not know. When your friend came here, her burn wounds were serious but not life-threatening. They could have treated her in the field hospital, but then they discovered she was pregnant, so they transferred her to Cologne. She would never have been in the field if anyone knew she was pregnant. She hid it well. We change her dressing every day, and she's isolated. Everyone entering this area wears a mask. The birth went smoothly. Yet, a day after giving birth, she was listless and developed a persistent fever. Her body healed at first but is succumbing to this infection. She has no fight left and her fever is always high."

"Perhaps I can, with love give her back a will – she might remember how loved she was, how beautiful."

"She's wasting away, we thought she would recover to protect the baby, but I am sad that it may be too late. If will were enough, I wager every one of the soldiers here would leave, return to a loving home, but their wounds are too deep. Many are dying. We wired you because she didn't want her husband to come; she seems afraid of him. When her fever reached 40 degrees, she was coherent and said you promised to raise her child. Georg Eddings' child. I suppose you are Mrs. Eddings, but you don't need to tell me. Despite her fears, we sent a telegram to her husband, but there's been no response. He'll be sorrowful the rest of his life if he doesn't forgive her now."

Sister Brigitte continued, "Let's not talk about this anymore today. You need to rest and think about caring for this boy, if her husband won't. We need to find a place for you to stay. There's a young man at the hospital who can take you to a hotel or to a flat where a local woman rents rooms. I don't know your situation; I don't want to influence you. Your friend's injury has kept us busy, and we are sympathetic, but we have so many wounded soldiers, and more every day. We certainly can't care for a baby, and we can only keep your friend until she heals."

If? Ilse thought.

Ilse rented a room in a baker's house rather than a hotel room. Ironically, there was no flour, and the baker's family was starving and a toddler squirmed and cried in hunger when she entered. The baker was fighting somewhere in France; his wife eagerly let out their bedroom and slept by the door with her three children. Better than to starve. When families visiting wounded soldiers needed a room she pocketed a few marks, and would buy an egg, a loaf, a few more potatoes. Ilse shared her dinner of watery potato soup with the landlady's children.

In the room, Ilse sat on the bed to think, to recall her friendship with Sara. Then the church bells chimed midnight and she cried out, "Save us, end this war, dear God."

On the way to the hospital in the morning, Ilse went into the cathedral and knelt during the Mass, though she did not take communion. She prayed for Georg, for Karl, for the young men on both sides, for their sacrifice and their suffering, and for the boys and girls turned into war slaves. She prayed for Sara and baby Paul—she'd name him Paul—until Sara healed.

While Ilse prayed, Sara's fever raged. When Ilse reached the hospital, she kissed her dead friend on the lips before Sara's body was removed.

Ilse could not sacrifice in the selfless way of the nurses and dress wounds, caring for patients continuously, how holy they were. Theirs was true charity. In war's horror, she could do at least one good deed, and she prayed she would learn to love the baby, for surely that was God's plan.

Ilse fervently believed this on the train back to Berlin, cradling and stroking a very ordinary baby, who was sometimes sleeping and sometimes crying and sometimes needed to be changed.

20

August 1999

Dana held up the flowers, for they were nodding, and said, "I hope Rachel will like these roses." and then she plunged the flowers in water.

Rachel had invited them to lunch.

The Eddingses apartment was light, a Juliet balcony made it attractive. These older buildings had fine architectural details. Only the mahogany furniture was dated, perhaps antique. Dana thought contemporary furniture would brighten it.

"Let's have lunch," Rachel said, putting the flowers in a Meissen vase. "These are my favorite flowers, I am so glad you brought them."

Everyone looked sporty, especially Gerson in a cheerful madras shirt. He had livened up, become almost cheerful, during the drive. A visit to someone's home was an adventure for both of them, they didn't get frequent weekend invitations.

Over chicken salad Paul and Gerson reminisced – Gerson remembering stories about his seven uncles, some rather eccentric.

"We called Uncle Fritz," he said, '*von und zu*,' he put on such airs. We always had to dress properly when he came. He was tall and slender, his wife was plump and very down to earth; she wore trousers and smoked. It was a very happy arranged marriage."

"I have heard about Gerson 's pranks, like pulling a chair out from under von und zu Uncle Fritz," Dana said.

In the living room, Paul said, "I brought these coins home especially to show you. These are coins my father gave me. For nearly eighty years I have preserved his gift and added to it. When he gave them to me I was seven, about to start my own collection. I wanted to share these with you, especially since you prize that necklace."

From a coin holder he took out a small coin and handed a loupe to each of them, "Here is a very fine example of the didrachm on your necklace. You can clearly see the head of Hercules on the front side, which numismatists call the obverse, and on the back, the reverse, the wolf nursing twins. The detailed descriptions were written by my father, to identify each coin. Below, you see catalogue numbers which I added from recent publications."

Didrachm, Sydenham 6, Crawford 20/1 Rome, 269-266 B.C

Passing two other coins to Gerson he continued, "This is a rather common coin minted by Julius Caesar, depicting Aeneas on the reverse and here's a bronze coin depicting Dido on the obverse."

Dana was fascinated by the coins, the designs, the way some were well centered and others not, and she tried, unsuccessfully, to decipher the Latin inscriptions. Mocking herself, she said, "Mr. Jacobs, my high school Latin teacher, would be displeased."

Taking another coin out of its holder, Paul said, "You don't need to handle these coins like crystal. Imagine how many hands held them since they were in the marketplace two thousand years ago. If you keep a napkin under them, there won't be any damage if they drop accidentally. I have always been fascinated by history and when I retired ten years ago, I began researching the circumstances of my parents' lives. I had some information, I knew that Sara Liebermann was my mother, but little about her. As you may imagine, by the time I was in high school in Germany researching my Jewish past was unthinkable. Even in retirement, it has taken me almost ten years to connect the dots. I had some information to start, but mostly my work in retirement has been a sort of dissertation on these intersecting lives. So you're my thesis committee."

"Dana said, "But we are only at the very beginning. Did you go to Catholic school? Did Ilse convert?"

"You will be surprised, after all I have told you, that Ilse postponed her conversion, she wouldn't hurt her parents. I went to the public school. I was a young boy; I had no idea about Ilse's religious crisis. At home, we were completely secular; at that time, it seemed a normal life to me, and my friends in school were mostly secular, too. Christmas and Easter included festivities without religious meaning. When Ilse and Georg went to church and Georg's parents to synagogue, which happened very rarely, it did not strike me as strange. I was too young to think much about it, and we rarely saw any family members from Munich. Until the Nazis came, the subject of being Jewish never came up."

"I hope you are continuing this research," Dana said.

"That is where I need your help," Paul said. "I need to do more sleuthing, but I am too old now, and I don't know Russian. Of course, I have engaged a consulting service to prepare a database list for me. You, young lady, are young and energetic, and you know Russian and you're probably very good at the computer. Will you continue what I began?"

"I'm confused. What has Russia to do with it?"

"When I was seven, Josif Jarecki, turned up in Berlin. Georg told us how he saved Josif's life," Paul sighed. "It was a barbaric time in Germany, there were rampages and murders, paramilitary units intimidated citizens, and barricades and battles took place right on our street. At that time Josif seemed my father's charismatic friend. I will never forget his face, his aquiline nose, set jaw, and gray-green eyes. I understood he was a revolutionary agitator, a leader in the Red Front. Berliners feared the right wing militias and they feared the Communists. Josif's friends were Radek and Thälmann, attempting to spur a proletarian revolution. Of course all this action in the streets was exciting for a young boy who didn't understand that the government was being destroyed. Josif mesmerized us, especially Ilse. In time she was in thrall to him, following him wherever he went, cooking for him, then living with him. This is where the story, as I know it, ends. Georg was anguished, and then threatened to kill himself. That I did not understand until much later. Ilse left for Russia with Josif when the Communists failed in Germany. There I lost the trail, because information was controlled and sequestered by the Soviets. Now those documents are declassified and if there is a God, together we will find out what happened to Ilse and to Josif. We might learn more about Sara, and her Russian family. Will you continue the research for us?"

"But I am not a scholar," Dana said. "I would not know how to begin."

Paul went out, and Dana was afraid she offended him. He came back from his library with two books, clearly a set.

"We'll do it together. Here's a bibliography of Russian archives, and I am already in touch with someone at the Russian National Library in Moscow. It will take time, but we can do this."

"All right," Dana said. Rachel was sitting near her and hugged her saying, "Thank you. Paul is fatigued; he cannot do much more of this. Wait, I too have something to give you, something much smaller."

Soon Rachel returned, with another coin holder and took out a silver coin. "Here," she said, is a gift for you. A nice coin of the Severan dynasty, about 200 AD. Here is a fine denarius with which you can begin a collection, if you wish. These coins are still affordable. You see we have faith in you and your many talents."

Dana marveled at how the lunch had turned out. She looked at her watch and realized it was late, but it had been worth it. She felt connected to Paul and Rachel. She looked at Gerson in a new way.

They drove home, both tired, but also exhilarated.

"For years," Gerson said, "I thought my family was responsible for Ilse's desertion and Paul being, as my mother said, abandoned. I have been ashamed for years, and today that changed. I blamed my family, especially my father, for Ilse and Georg's pain. What was my father's *emunah*[*], if it made life intolerable for Ilse and Georg and Paul? I realize now he wasn't guiltless, but that wasn't the whole truth. My father was, mostly, a good man."

The car swept up the dirt road, and when they reached the house, the three dogs were panting, running in circles around them.

It was dark, Dana turned on a flashlight and she and Gerson walked up to the house together.

He continued, "For years I could not speak of this, now I feel released. You can help, Dana."

"Ah, alone no. But with you, yes." Dana said.

They slowed and held hands, listening to the rippling stream and night birds calling their mates.

After dinner they spoke of misled heretics and Communists taken in by false promises. They glimpsed themselves visiting libraries and archives, researching, attending conferences, fulfilling Paul's quest.

At night, half dreaming, Dana heard Ilse, Georg and Sara calling to her, "We trust you and thank you."

---

[*] *Emunah* - faith

Dana hadn't prayed since she was in school or even given much thought to God, yet she imagined *zayde* Isaac dancing with the Torah in the Putnam Valley synagogue, a simple wooden ranch house. She accepted this as an affirmation.

At daybreak, she opened her drawer, seized her coin necklace and danced with it.

Families in Germany

Ehrenkrantz:
>Moshe and Hedwig Ehrenkrantz of Munich
>
>Their children:
>Walther
>Leon
>Ilse
>Annette

Eddings (originally Ettinger):
>Werther and Lottie Eddings of Berlin
>(Lottie is Moshe's sister and Werther's second wife)
>Georg, Werther's son from a first marriage

Neumann/Newman
>Neumann family of Hamburg
>Martin, one of eight brothers, moves to Munich

Liebermann
>Max and Sara Liebermann of Munich
>(Klara, Max's deceased first wife)
>Dorothea, Max's daughter from first marriage

Bertram
    Claude Bertram, university student and piano teacher
    French citizen who returns with his mother to France at outbreak
of WWI

Appendix: Names of cities and transliteration

Where possible, the names of German places are used as in Standard English. For foreign words, I have followed The Library of Congress transliteration system.

Postscript

The Numismatist's Wife is a fictional work, with invented names, characters, and dialogue. Liberties have been taken with events, places, and dates, and any resemblance to actual persons, living or dead, is purely coincidental. While writing and revising, I read and reread novels by Virginia Woolf, A.S. Byatt, Michel Faber and Helen MacDonald. Where there is a clear use of a source, I want to make the allusion obvious; for example, the phrase "If it's fine tomorrow" appears in the opening section of Woolf's *To the Lighthouse*. The germ of Moshe's tale of rebbetzen is from Bulgakov's *The Master and Margarita*, and the character of Adriana has some features of Sugar from *The Crimson Petal and White*. Aleksander Solzhenitsyn's *November 1916* changed my perspective on Russia during World War I.

I have taken some liberties with the facts; thus, my characters would not have been able to reach Bad Kötzting, hike there, and return to Munich in one day. There has never been a Camaldolese Convent in Venice, and General Bielenberg is an invented character. Newsreels of the war were not prevalent in Germany before 1915. The headmistress of Burano's lacemaking school was Signora Marcetti, but the organization and appearance of the school are invented.

From the first time I saw Franz Marc's paintings, I have been in awe of the image of blue horses. Ezra Pound's correspondence was a source of hours of enjoyable reading, as was Virginia Woolf's correspondence. Tom Holland's *Dynasty* is a beautifully written history of Roman times, and my characters would have been delighted with his chapter on Augustus.

Tony Tanner's *Venice Desired* elucidates Proust's fascination with Venice and Pound's scholarly interest and translation of Catullus.

For the German soldiers' encounter with Eastern Europe I recommend Richard Dehmel's <u>Zwischen Volk und Menschheit – Kriegstagebuch</u>, Robert L. Nelson's <u>German Soldier Newspapers of the First World War</u> and Vejas Gabriel Liulevicius' <u>War Land on the Eastern Front</u>.

Acknowledgments

I am indebted to the rabbis of the Upper West Side, New York City, who were my mentors. I learned much from their courses and talks. Any errors are solely mine. The Leo Baeck Institute was a welcoming environment that provided context for some of the material, and I am especially grateful to Michael Simonson for his patience and support while I was engrossed in the writing of this novel, as well as for his assistance with digital images. A special thank you to Prof. Polly Zavadivker for permission to quote lines from her translation of <u>1915 Diary of S. Ansky: A Russian Jewish Writer at the Front</u>. Lois Spatz gave me helpful suggestions on the classics. I greatly benefited from Professor Paul Kaplan's course on Albrecht Dürer. I would also like to thank Angelika Leissl for her assistance with German terms and customs; Scott Rottinghaus, without whose numismatic advice I would have been unable to write sections of this book; and the American Numismatic Society (ANS) for its valuable 2010 Summer Seminar. Olaf Olsen prompted me to increase my knowledge of trains of the period, and as a result, I have learned from Lucius's Beebe's wonderful illustrated books on steam trains. Thanks to Florence Boos, Renee Cafiero, Michelle Caplan, Robert Kramer, Sebastian Laudan, Chuck Muckle, Ross Perlin, Carolyn Prager, Lance Ringel, Lottie Salton and Louise Smith for suggestions, mentoring and friendship.

Unless otherwise noted, translations from the Book of Exodus, Psalm 91, I Corinthians and the Book of Revelation are taken from the King James Version.

Many libraries were generous with their materials, especially the

Watson Library of the Metropolitan Museum, the Avery Arts Library at Columbia University, and the Zentralarchiv der Staatlichen Museen zu BerlinPreußischer Kulturbesitz. The diligent staff of the Arts and Architecture Library and Library of the Performing Arts of the New York Public Library was untiring in retrieving books for me. In addition, I'd especially like to express my deep appreciation to David Hill, Francis D. Campbell librarian at the American Numismatic Society, and to the American Numismatic Society for help in my research over the years.

Most importantly, for as long as she was able, my mother, Esther Karpman z"l, who passed away in 2016, was my most loyal reader. I hope she would have been pleased with this novel. I thank my father, Itzhak Karpman z"l, who came from Bjekow, for his love and support. The families of both my parents were killed by the Nazis in Poland.

Dahlia Japhet
New York, New York

Permissions

COVER: Menzel, Adolph von, Living Room with the Artist's Sister. 1847. Photo Credit: bpk Bildagentur/Neue Pinakothek, Art Resource, New York

p.13 – Courtesy, American Numismatic Society, accessed July 7, 2017 http://numismatics.org/collections/1950.148.2

p.19 – Courtesy, Munchner Stadtmuseum, Sammlung Fotografie, Archiv Kester

p.39 - Harvard Art Museums/Arthur M. Sackler Museum, Bequest of Frederick M. Watkins, 1972.134 Photo: Imaging Department © President and Fellows of Harvard College

p.104 - Courtesy American Numismatic Society, accessed July 7, 2017 http://numismatic.org/collections/1944.100.38341

p.117 - Courtesy, National World War I Museum and Memorial, Kansas City, Missouri, USA https://the worldwar.org/explore/online-collections-database

p.119 - Courtesy, Leo Baeck Institute

p.120 - Courtesy, National World War I Museum and Memorial, Kansas City, Missouri, USA https://the worldwar.org/explore/online-collections-database p.146 - Courtesy Metropolitan Museum of Art, open access, public domain

p.147 - Courtesy, Metropolitan Museum of Art, open access, public domain

p.148 - Courtesy, Metropolitan Museum of Art, open access, public domain

p.155 - From the Bernhard Bardach Collection. Courtesy of the Leo Baeck Institute.

p.156 - From the Bernhard Bardach Collection. Courtesy of the Leo Baeck Institute.

p.169 - Cover and this image author's collection, photographed by Scott Rottinghaus